LIGHT OF THE MOON

The Marquis' voice deepened as he spoke:
"Have I spoilt what you felt for me, my precious?"

Neoma moved a little nearer to him.

"I am ... sure that if you ... kiss me ... we will find it is still there."

She only whispered the words, but the Marquis heard them.

He put his arms out, she moved into them, and he held her very gently against him.

"Oh, my little light of the Moon," he cried. "Having found you, I think it would kill me if I lost you!"

"That is ... how I felt ... when I thought I had ... lost you."

The Marquis drew her closer and slowly, as if he were half-afraid, his lips found hers.

Just for one agonising moment Neoma thought that the wonder she had felt was gone. Then like a streak of lightning running through her it was there—moving through her whole body into her heart ...

Bantam books by Barbara Cartland
Ask your bookseller for the books you have missed

Barbara Cartland's Library of Love series

Barbara Cartland's Ancient Wisdom series

Other Books by Barbara Cartland

RECIPES FOR LOVERS

Barbara Cartland
Light of the Moon

BANTAM BOOKS
TORONTO · NEW YORK · LONDON

LIGHT OF THE MOON
A Bantam Book | May 1979

ISBN 0–553–12785–3

Published simultaneously in the United States and Canada

Bantam Books are published by Bantam Books, Inc. Its trade-
mark, consisting of the words "Bantam Books" and the por-
trayal of a bantam, is Registered in U.S. Patent and Trademark
Office and in other countries. Marca Registrada. Bantam
Books, Inc., 666 Fifth Avenue, New York, New York 10019.

PRINTED IN THE UNITED STATES OF AMERICA

Author's Note

Derby Day, from its inception in 1780, assumed such importance that Disraeli called the Derby Stakes "the Blue Ribbon of the Turf."

In 1847, because the Members of the House of Commons wanted to be present on the Downs, a motion proposed that the House should "take the day off." This was passed with only a few Scottish Members voting against it.

There has always been a Royal connection with the race. The Duke of Cumberland's *Eclipse* was an "also ran" in the first Derby, in 1788 the Prince of Wales (later George IV) won the race with *Sir Thomas,* who was the favourite. But the most exciting was when Edward VII became the first reigning Monarch to win with *Minoru.* The entire crowd burst into the National Anthem.

Chapter One

1820

"I'm sorry, Miss, I am reelly! I didn't mean t' do it."

The voice was tearful and Neoma as she looked ruefully at the scorched table-cloth forced herself to say quietly:

"It is all right, Emily. It was not your fault. I should have ironed it myself."

"I were only a-trying t' help, Miss; you knows I wants to please you."

"Yes, I know. You try very hard, Emily."

"It's just that I can't do things th' way you tells me."

Now the tears overflowed and ran down the girl's face.

"You do a lot of things very well," Neoma said, "and you are getting better every day, so let us forget the table-cloth. It is an old one."

"I'll try to do better in future, I reelly will, Miss," Emily said, wiping the tears from her eyes with the back of her hand.

"I am sure you will," Neoma said, "and now finish cleaning the kitchen-floor. Then I can start cooking the luncheon. I am sure Mr. Peregrine will be home soon."

Picking up the scorched table-cloth, Neoma left the room and took it upstairs to the linen-cupboard.

1

It would come in for patching, she told herself, and hoped that Emily would not try to help her another time, for it invariably ended in disastrous consequences.

It was not the girl's fault. She was only fourteen and had come to the house completely untrained.

As Neoma knew only too well, they could not afford older and more experienced servants, and she just had to hope that Emily would soon get over the phase of breaking and somehow contriving to ruin everything she touched.

It had been the same with Annie, but as soon as Annie was fairly proficient in her duties, she realised that she could get a great deal more money elsewhere, and Neoma had to start again with another young girl.

As she reached the linen-cupboard at the top of the stairs she told herself that she was lucky to have anyone to help her. After all, the house was so small and it was not like living at the Manor.

At the same time, even to think of her home in the country brought a yearning expression to Neoma's face.

How she missed the house in which she had lived ever since she was a child. How she longed for the garden, which even if it was overgrown was always a picture of beauty at this time of the year, with the lilacs and the syringas in bloom!

The first roses would now be coming into bud in the rose-garden which had been her mother's delight. But it was no use thinking about Standish Manor, Neoma told herself.

Peregrine wanted to be in London and who could blame him? Life in the country for young gentlemen without money and without good horses was exceedingly dull.

Neoma opened the linen-cupboard, folded the damaged table-cloth, and put it neatly away on the shelf where she kept the linen which was no longer of any use.

The shelf was becoming full and she thought, with

a little sigh, that so many sheets, towels, and pillow-
cases which they had used at home were gradually
getting old and dilapidated.

But there was still quite a pile of linen on the
other shelves and she told herself that it would be a
long time before they had to buy anything new.

"And if we did, where would the money come
from?" asked a voice in her mind.

It was a question which occurred not once but a
dozen times a day and it had always made Neoma shiver.

It was so difficult to manage with the minute
amount of money that Peregrine allowed her for the
housekeeping in London.

In the country there had been vegetables from
the garden, rabbits and pigeons when anybody could
be persuaded to shoot them, and of course freshly
laid eggs.

All these now had to be bought, and she was
not surprised when Peregrine would exclaim disgusted-
ly that the food did not taste as it used to and ask
what was the matter with her cooking.

There was no use explaining to him that her
cooking was just the same; it was that she could not
afford to buy from any but the cheapest shops or off
the barrows which were always to be found in King's
Road:

They had been lucky about one thing—the house
they had rented in Chelsea was small and furnished.

The previous occupant, Neoma had discovered,
was an actress and the house had been provided for
her by a gentleman who had also furnished it.

Neoma did not understand the relationship between the actress and the gentleman; in fact it rather
puzzled her, and for some reason which she could not
ascertain, they had quarrelled and the actress had
moved to larger and richer premises.

This had been fortunate for Neoma and Peregrine, who had been able to rent the house for quite
a small sum of money while the gentleman's Solici-
tors were endeavouring to sell it.

"Of course I shall not wish to bring my friends

back here," Peregrine had said in a lofty tone. "Any
entertaining I need to do shall be at my Club."

"Entertaining?"

Neoma had been hardly able to breathe the word
before she cried:

"Peregrine, you cannot afford to entertain! You
known how little money we have."

"That is all very well," he replied swiftly, "but
if I accept hospitality I ought to make some effort
to return it."

"Not if you cannot afford to pay!" Neoma said
firmly. "Whatever happens, dearest, you must not run
up debts. That would be fatal!"

Peregrine had not been pleased at her admonish-
ing him so often about their penniless position.

Because Neoma loved her brother and wished to
make him happy, she had, with difficulty, forborne
from saying that he could not afford it when he insisted on coming to London.

It had been hard enough to find the clothes that
Peregrine wanted, since he had grandoise ideas that
he must go to a fashionable tailor and of course wear
the close-fitting champagne-coloured pantaloons which
were all the rage amongst the Bucks of St. James's
Street.

He also required what seemed to be an abnormal
number of muslin cravats, which had to be washed
and stiffened in exactly the right manner and tied in
what was the very latest fashion.

Neoma had learnt why such a large number were
required when Peregrine, since he had no valet, would
ruin over half-a-dozen, perhaps more, before he managed to tie one to his satisfaction.

Because of all the time spent in pressing and
starching, Neoma practised alone until she could
perfect styles which Peregrine had told her were the
vogue.

At first he was very scornful of her insistence
that she should try to tie his cravat as he wished it
to be done.

But when he saw the result, he merely asked
his sister to learn a number of other styles, which

eventually, he told her, made him the envy of his friends.

"Charles asked me who my new valet was," he told Neoma.

"Charles knows perfectly well that you cannot afford a valet," Neoma replied, "so he was either being sarcastic or paying me a somewhat obscure compliment!"

"I have no intention of telling Charles that you tie my cravats," Peregrine said. "You know what a gossip he is."

"That is true," Neoma replied, laughing, "so he must just think you tie them yourself and are very clever at doing so."

"That is exactly what I intend him to think!" Peregrine said firmly.

Charles Waddesdon was Peregrine's closest friend. As children they had played together because their estates marched with each other's.

They had gone to Eton together, and although Charles, who had inherited his father's Baronetcy and impoverished estate, had intended to go to Oxford, when he found that Peregrine was unable to do so, they had decided that they would introduce themselves to London instead.

Sometimes Neoma wondered if it would not have been better to try by some desperate means to find enough money for Peregrine to go up to Oxford.

But it was too late now, and she had been appalled at the amount of expenditure which was incurred in fitting her brother out as a "Gentleman of Fashion."

However, what she really minded was having to shut up their home.

Granted, they had lived in only a few rooms and she had had to manage the whole house with just an old couple who had been in her father and mother's service for over forty years.

The couple had stayed to caretake because somebody had to look after the house, and Neoma, coping now with a half-witted girl, missed their slow but thorough manner of doing things.

She also missed being able to talk to them about her father and mother and the "old days."

That had been a very frequent subject and Neoma never got tired of hearing of the parties at which her mother was the hostess or the Hunt-Breakfasts when her father was Master of the Hounds.

There had been a great many servants in the past to help run the Manor.

There had been six gardeners to make the lawns look like velvet and keep the shrubs under control but wild and untrained, and the gardens flourished in a manner that, Neoma thought, made it one of the most beautiful places on earth.

Every shaft of sunlight that came through the windows in Royal Avenue made her long to be back where, she told herself, she "belonged."

But there was Peregrine to be considered, and her brother wanted all the excitement and gaiety that was to be found in London.

At the thought of him Neoma glanced at the clock in the Hall and wondered what had happened and where he could have stayed the night.

She felt sure that it would have been at Charles Waddesdon's apartments in Half Moon Street.

It was where Peregrine had stayed several times before, when, to be honest, he had been too "foxed" to make the journey back to Chelsea.

Neoma told herself in a practical manner that that was what had happened last night. At the same time, she could not help worrying simply because Peregrine was so reckless and unpredictable.

"I will cook him a really nice luncheon," she told herself.

She was just starting to walk down the stairs when she heard his knock on the front door.

It was a sound different from that made by anybody else, and Neoma gave a little cry of delight and ran down the stairs.

She opened the front door to find Peregrine, as she had expected, standing on the door-step, still in his evening-clothes and with the cravat she had so skilfully tied for him looking limp and creased.

There was also an expression on his face which made her draw in her breath.

"What is it?" she asked. "What has happened?"

To her surprise, her brother pushed past her without answering, threw his top-hat down on a chair in the narrow Hallway, and said harshly:

"I want to talk to you, Neoma!"

He walked ahead into the Sitting-Room at the back of the house.

It faced what Neoma thought scornfully was nothing more than a yard, but there was a large crab-apple tree in it and the blossoms compensated for the ugliness of the backs of the buildings, which was the only view there was from the window.

As she followed Peregrine into the Sitting-Room she shut the door behind her, and as he stood with his back to the empty fireplace she saw that he had had a very bad night.

He looked pale, there were dark lines under his eyes, and she thought that he had obviously been drinking to excess, as he had done on previous occasions.

It was certainly one of the hazards of having come to London.

Peregrine had never drunk very much in the country; in fact he had not really cared for claret. But now, because it was the thing to do, he drank with the gentlemen he met in his Club and invariably it made him feel ill the next day.

Because she was very perceptive where Peregrine was concerned, as Neoma waited for him to speak, she felt that it was not only drunkenness that had upset him but something else.

Something, she felt with a sudden constriction of her heart, which might be disastrous.

"I have something to tell you," Peregrine said.

"What is it, dearest?" Neoma enquired. "Could it not wait until after you have had some coffee? It will only take me a minute to get you a pot."

"I have to tell you before I do anything else," Peregrine said in an obstinate tone which told her that it was no use arguing with him.

Neoma sat down on one of the chairs and looked up at him expectantly.

"I do not know how to begin," he said after a moment.

"Start at the beginning," Neoma replied. "When you left here yesterday evening you told me that you and Charles were going to spend the evening together."

"That is what we did," Peregrine answered. "I picked up Charles at his rooms and we went to White's."

It was the smartest Club in St. James's and the haunt of all the most important Bucks and Beaux. Neoma knew that Peregrine and Charles thought themselves extremely fortunate to have been elected Members.

This had been due to the fact that both his father and Charles's had been Members and there had therefore been no difficulty in getting themselves accepted by the Committee.

Also, as Peregrine had pointed out to his sister, as they were completely unknown in London, there was nobody likely to blackball them.

Because the Members of White's were celebrated for hard gambling and hard drinking, Neoma had often wondered if it would have been better if Peregrine had joined a less fashionable Club.

Whenever they had nowhere else to go, he and Charles went to White's, where they could always find a number of kindred spirits to drink with them.

"When we reached White's," Peregrine went on, "we had a small dinner, then went up to the Card-Room."

Neoma drew in her breath.

Now she was afraid . . . very afraid of what Peregrine was going to tell her.

"There were a lot of people playing for high stakes," he went on, "and when one of them won a really large amount of money, he stood drinks all round."

"Is that usual?" Neoma enquired.

"It does not happen as often as one would like," Peregrine said with a grin.

"Go on!" she prompted.

"After that, everybody got rather generous-minded, and Charles and I had a lot of free drinks one way or another. Then we got bored with watching the play."

"So what did you do?"

"We sat down and played Piquet with each other."

"That sounds rather sensible," Neoma said in an encouraging voice.

"It was something we had done before," her brother replied. "When we think people are watching us, we have an arrangement by which we pretend to win or lose large sums of money."

"What do you mean?" Neoma asked.

"Well, we say aloud that we will bet so much on each game, so much for each point," Peregrine explained; "then, whoever loses writes the other an IOU. It is a sensible thing to do when everybody else is gambling so high."

Neoma could understand exactly what they felt.

Because they were both so young—Peregrine would not be twenty until December and Charles was the same age—they wanted to show off in front of their friends or anyone else who noticed them.

It was the sort of pretence in which they had indulged in all sorts of different ways ever since they were small boys.

She remembered that at one time they had both pretended to own race-horses, and after each important race-meeting they would talk quite solemnly of the prize-money they had won and work out the increased value of their horses.

"What happened?" she asked now.

"We had been playing for some time and drinking quite a lot," Peregrine answered, "when there was an empty place at the card-table next to ours and a Club servant came to ask:

" 'Would either of you gentlemen care to take a hand?'

"I shook my head, but to my astonishment Charles said:

" 'I will play! I feel in a winning mood tonight.'

"Then as he rose and walked towards the table, I realised that he was foxed."

Neoma looked at her brother apprehensively, but she did not interrupt as Peregrine went on:

"Charles sat down. Somebody told him the stakes, and to my horror he wrote a chit for quite a large sum of money."

"Is that something you can do at the Club?" Neoma asked.

"Of course!" Peregrine said impatiently. "Members do not carry that sort of money about with them."

Neoma gave a little sigh, and her brother continued:

"I went up to Charles and whispered in his ear: 'Are you mad? You cannot play with money you do not possess. Say you feel ill and come away.' "

"What did he reply?" Neoma asked.

"He would not listen to me," Peregrine said, "and instantly he ordered a drink!"

"Oh, Peregrine!" Neoma exclaimed.

Although Charles Waddeson was the fifth Baronet, he had almost as little money as she and Peregrine had.

His father had lost his fortune during the war, just as their money had disappeared in rents that were never paid and in shares where the interest decreased and decreased until it gradually vanished.

Both Charles and Peregrine owned country houses, farms which needed large sums of money spent on them to make them properly productive, and quite a number of acres of land which were unfarmable.

"I knew that Charles was drunk," Peregrine was saying, "but even when he is like that he appears to be completely in control of himself. Only somebody who knows him as well as I do would realise that he is living in a fantasy which has no contact with reality."

"In other words," Neoma said in a low voice, "he was actually believing that he was rich and was behaving accordingly."

"Exactly!" Peregrine agreed. "And he began to gamble in a manner which terrified me."

"What did he do?"

"He staked astronomical sums, at least that is what they seemed to me, but to the other people at the table I suppose it was a quite commonplace amount of money."

"Why would he not listen to you?" Neoma cried.

"I do not think he even heard what I was saying to him," Peregrine replied, "and of course I had to speak in a whisper. I did not want the other people at the table to know that he was making a fool of himself."

"How much did he lose?" Neoma asked, knowing how the story must end and feeling that she could not bear not to hear the worst.

"He won!"

"Won?" Neoma exclaimed.

"To begin with," Peregrine said. "In fact he seemed to have a magic touch. Everything went his way and he won and won!"

"Oh, Peregrine!"

A feeling of relief swept over Neoma like a wave from the sea.

"I could hardly believe I was not dreaming," Peregrine said. "Then I knew that I had to get Charles away while he was still a winner."

"That was sensible of you."

"When he would not listen to my whispers," Peregrine continued, "I begged him to stop. I said aloud: 'Do not forget, Charles, that we have an engagement to keep at midnight. We will be late as it is!' "

Neoma looked at him approvingly as he went on:

"Charles behaved as if he had not heard me. In fact, he brushed me aside in a way that told me he was even drunker than I had thought."

Neoma waited. She felt as if she already knew the end of the story.

"Then Charles began to lose. At one moment he

must have had nine or ten thousand pounds in front of him, but it began to dwindle.

" 'Come away, Charles! Do come away!' I begged.

"But he had a kind of wild glint in his eye, which gamblers get when nothing else matters and they see nothing except the cards on the table."

"Did he ... lose it ... all?" Neoma asked in a low voice.

"Worse than that," Peregrine said. "He had on the table, with the IOUs of the other players, about four thousand pounds. Then a man opposite began to bid against him. I was not certain who it was at first, then I realised that it was the Marquis of Rosyth."

"Who is he?" Neoma asked.

"One of the most frightening people I have ever met," Peregrine replied, "but I will tell you about him later."

"Of course. Go on!" Neoma begged.

"I heard the bidding rising and rising," Peregrine said. "Suddenly Charles stopped. The cards were turned and he had lost!"

"Oh ... Peregrine!"

"It was then, as Charles seemed to sink lower in his chair, that the Marquis said:

" 'I think, Sir Charles, you owe me six thousand pounds!'

"I gasped because I did not think that Charles had as much in front of him, but he pulled some notes from his pocket, flung them down on the rest of the money, and said:

" 'That is all I have, My Lord, and now my pockets are "to let"!' "

Peregrine paused, then he added:

"I think everybody realised by this time that Charles was foxed, if they were not already aware of it, because he collapsed and closed his eyes."

"What ... happened ... then?"

"The Marquis drew the money towards him and deliberately, in what I felt was a contemplative manner, counted the notes and sovereigns. Then he said:

" 'It appears to be the right amount, so I must thank you, Sir Charles, for an excellent game.'

"Charles revived at that, and with what I knew was an effort to sound indifferent he said:

" 'I—enjoyed it—too, My Lord.'

"The Marquis looked up and I had the feeling that he knew that Charles was play-acting. He seemed to look us over in a hard manner which I at once resented, and then he said:

" 'I feel I ought to give you a chance to take your revenge. Why do not both you young men come and stay with me for the Derby?' "

Peregrine paused, then he said:

"Charles was as surprised as I was, and before I could speak he stammered:

" 'That is very—kind of—Your Lordship, and it will give me great pleasure to be your guest.'

" 'And you,' the Marquis said, looking at me, 'I am not quite certain of your name.'

" 'It is Standish, My Lord. Peregrine Standish.'

" 'I would like you to accompany Waddesdon,' the Marquis said, 'and as it is a mixed party, I suggest that each of you bring a lady-friend, or perhaps that is giving a somewhat grandiose name to the type of guest I envisage. I am sure you must be acquainted with some attractive "bits o' muslin".' "

"What did he mean?" Neoma asked.

"That was what I wondered for a moment," Peregrine replied, "then before I could say any more, the Marquis rose, saying:

" 'I shall expect you at Syth the day after tomorrow, at about five o'clock, accompanied of course by the fair charmers who will undoubtedly enliven the solemnity of the racing!' Then he was gone!"

"I do not . . . understand . . . ." Neoma began, but Peregrine interrupted her.

"You have not heard the end."

"What else . . . happened?"

"Charles was sober enough to be extremely gratified by having an invitation to stay with anyone as important as the Marquis of Rosyth. At the same time,

while his brain could take it in, his legs were unsteady.
I got him downstairs and we took a hackney-carriage
to his lodgings. When I got him to his room, he sat
down on the bed and said:

" 'God, Peregrine, I have got a head!'

" 'Serves you right!' I replied. 'If you had not
been such a fool you could have come away with perhaps eight thousand pounds!'

" 'Did I really win as much as that?' Charles asked
in a bewildered tone.

" 'At least eight thousand,' I said. 'I am sure it
was more at one time.'

" 'Why did I not listen to you?' he said, groaning.

" 'Because you were completely foxed,' I answered, 'although I suppose I ought to be fair and say
you would not have played at all if you had not been
under the hatches.'

"I wanted to be angry with him," Peregrine went
on, "but somehow it was impossible. You know what
Charles is like. He just put his head in his hand and
groaned, and I knew he was thinking what a cork-brain
he had been and what a difference it would have made
to both of us if he had eight thousand pounds to play
with."

"Well, at least there is no harm done," Neoma
said.

She realised how worried and apprehensive she
had been when Peregrine had started his tale.

"I still have not finished," her brother replied.

"I am sorry, dearest," Neoma apologised. "Go on!"

" 'The only blessing in the whole affair,' I said
to Charles," Peregrine continued, " 'is that you had
enough money to pay the Marquis. For one awful
moment I thought you were going to be nearly two
thousand pounds short, until you produced some notes
from your pocket.'

" 'There was not that amount of money there,'
Charles murmured. 'Just what I had to live on until
the next quarter.'

" 'I rather fancied that,' I said, 'but I suppose
things might have been worse.'

"Charles was silent for quite a long time, then he said suddenly:

" 'Peregrine! I have just had an awful thought!'

" 'What is it?' I asked.

"He started to feel in his coat-pockets, pulling out his handkerchief, some visiting-cards, and a snuff-box which he carries but never uses. As you know, neither Charles nor I like snuff."

"What was he looking for?" Neoma asked.

"I did not realise what it was for a moment," Peregrine said. "Then as Charles looked at me, there was no need for words."

"Why not?" Neoma asked, mystified.

"Slowly he drew from his waist-coat pocket the IOUs I had given him when we were playing Piquet," Peregrine said dramatically. "There were only two, and I remembered that I had written a third just before the Club servant interrupted our game."

Neoma drew in her breath and waited for the blow to fall.

"For two thousand pounds!" Peregrine said in a voice that shook.

"You mean . . . Charles had . . . given it to the . . . Marquis?"

"Exactly! He had not put it in the same waist-coat pocket in which he had put the others, but in his trouser-pocket with his money. That was why the Marquis said the amount that he had won was right!"

"Oh . . . Peregrine!"

Neoma's exclamation was a cry of sheer horror. Then, before her brother could speak, she said:

"But surely it is quite easy. You only have to go to the Marquis and explain that it was a mistake."

"He will still expect Charles to make good on the money."

Neoma wanted to say that that was Charles's problem, but she knew that she could not do so.

Charles was in the same impecunious state that they were, and besides, she knew that gambling-debts were ones of honour.

Her father had so often told her of the tragedies

which occurred when men lost enormous sums at the
tables and caused their wives and families to suffer miserably in consequence.

Where a gentleman was concerned there were no
appeals against such losses, and she knew too that if
there were any difficulties over a payment, the loser
would be obliged to resign from his Club.

Nevertheless, because she was so desperately
shocked at what Peregrine had told her, she said:

"Surely Charles ... realises that he is ... liable?"

"Of course he does!" Peregrine answered. "But
you know that he cannot raise two thousand pounds
any more than I can."

"Will he try?"

"I have a better idea."

"What is that?"

"We sat up all night talking about it, and I can
assure you," her brother replied, "that Charles sobered
up quick enough when he realised what had happened."

"I was worried about what had happened to you,"
Neoma said in a quiet voice.

"I was worried myself," Peregrine retorted bitterly. "But there is only one hope."

"And what is that?"

"That the Marquis will not demand payment from
me until the usual week has elapsed."

"A week!"

"It can sometimes be two."

"It would not matter if it was nine hundred and
two," Neoma said. "You know you cannot find two
thousand pounds!"

"I know that," her brother retorted. "So listen
to what I am trying to say to you, Neoma."

"I am sorry, dearest, but naturally I am upset."

"You can hardly think that I am dancing for
joy! And Charles is in absolute despair. He is in debt
and he long ago sold everything in his house that was
saleable."

Neoma knew that this was true, and it certainly
did not make things any better.

With an effort she forced herself to ask calmly:

"What is your idea, dearest? Please tell me about it."

"Charles and I have decided," Peregrine said, "that we must somehow steal back the IOU!"

"Steal?" Neoma cried.

She spoke so loudly that her voice seemed to echo round the small room.

"Now listen to me!" Peregrine said. "Before you start being hysterical, I have to tell you about the Marquis."

"I am . . . listening."

At the same time, she clenched her hands together to prevent herself from saying a great deal more.

"He is hard, he is ruthless, and nobody likes him," Peregrine began. "It is well known that he enjoys winning at cards and does not care who suffers in consequence."

Neoma wanted to say that this was not a plausible excuse for stealing, but she managed to remain silent as Peregrine went on:

"They all say that the Marquis is the most unpopular man in White's simply because he has never given anybody a kind word. Also, since he is extremely lucky at cards, a great number of people have lost whole fortunes to him."

"Why is he so unpleasant?"

"It is not exactly that he is unpleasant," Peregrine answered. "He never raises his voice and they say he is never rude. But he just rides rough-shod through the world, completely regardless of anybody else's feelings."

He gave a little laugh but there was no humour in it.

"And there is no reason why he should be considerate. He is very important and exceedingly rich. He owns the most fabulous houses, and his horses win every Classic race."

"Of course! That is where I have heard his name!" Neoma said. "When you and Charles were playing your racing-game, I recall you saying that your imaginary horses had beaten the Marquis of Rosyth's."

"I suppose he has won almost every important race there is," Peregrine said, "and that does not make people like him any the better."

"I expect they are jealous."

"I am not jealous, but I hate him!"

Neoma waited for her brother to explain, and he went on:

"He is too experienced not to have known that Charles was drunk, and when I look back on the game I can see that he incited him to go on playing and, particularly at the last, to bid higher and higher."

"Do you really think the Marquis knew that Charles was not in complete possession of his senses?" Neoma asked.

"Of course he knew!" Peregrine replied. "He would have had to be deaf and blind not to know that I was trying to persuade Charles to come away from the table!"

"Then I agree with you, he is despicable!"

"I thought you would think so," Peregrine said, "and that is why you have to help us."

"I . . . help . . . you?" Neoma said with a gasp. "How can I . . . do that?"

Peregrine sat down on the chair nearest his sister's and said:

"I knew you would be shocked at our idea of stealing back the IOU, and I said to Charles: 'Neoma will not like this.' "

"Of course I do not like it!" Neoma said. "It is something, Peregrine, which you must not do. How could you of all people steal?"

"I have to! I have to get back that IOU. There is no other way, because it is no use pretending for one moment that either Charles or I could pay."

"When the Marquis finds that it is gone, will he not suspect you?"

"Even if he does, how can he possibly accuse us if we are staying in his house as his guests?" Peregrine replied.

Neoma wanted to say that if the Marquis was as bad as her brother said he was, he would undoubtedly

accuse them and even bring them to Court, but she
thought it best to keep silent as Peregrine went on:

"I told you, the Marquis invited us to stay and
we accepted. He also expects us each to bring a woman.
That is all right for Charles. He can bring Avril."

"Who is Avril?"

"An actress with whom he is rather taken. She
is genuinely fond of Charles and will do anything he
asks of her, but I have no-one I could take—but you!"

Neoma gasped and Peregrine went on quickly:

"I know it is not the sort of party to which you
should go, but even if I knew of a woman, I could not
afford to pay her."

"Pay her?" Neoma echoed in astonishment.
"Why should you pay someone to go to a party with
you?"

Peregrine looked away from her and she had a
feeling that he was not going to tell her the truth.

"There is no need for me to answer that question," he said after a moment, "for the simple reason
that you have to come with me. You are clever,
Neoma, and perhaps you will find a chance to get
back the IOU for Charles and I will not have any
chance at all."

"If you think I am going to steal for you," Neoma
said, "you are very much mistaken! I do not accept
for one moment that that is the only solution to your
problem."

"All right," Peregrine said. "You think of another. Charles and I sat up all night trying to find an
alternative."

Neoma was silent.

The only real solution, she knew, was for them
to pay their debt, but how could they possibly do
that?

It seemed to her as she thought of it, that the
bit of paper with Peregrine's signature on it seemed
to get larger and larger.

"Supposing the Marquis . . . catches you . . . stealing from him?" she said at length, weakly. "What do
you think will . . . happen?"

"There is one alternative," Peregrine said. "I am only surprised that you have not thought of it."

"What is it?" Neoma asked.

"We could try to find a buyer for the Manor, or just hand it over to the Marquis instead of money."

"Sell . . . the Manor?"

Neoma's voice was barely above a whisper.

"In its present condition I doubt if it is worth two thousand pounds."

"Of course it is worth that—and a great deal more!" she said indignantly.

"I will tell you something," Peregrine said, "but you must swear not to tell anybody."

"No, of course not."

"Charles tried to sell his house when we decided to come to London. He thought it would be more fun to have decent lodgings or perhaps buy a small house."

"What happened?" Neoma asked, already knowing the answer.

"He did not find a single purchaser. Nobody wants dilapidated houses in the country at this moment, and you know as well as I do that empty farms are a glut on the market."

That was true, Neoma knew.

The farmers who had been praised and considered so important to the war, when they were producing food during Napoleon's attempt to blockade England, were now going bankrupt one after the other.

The Banks refused them any further loans, the Government ignored their cries for help, and cheaper food than they could produce was being imported from the Continent.

Two small farms on their own estate, Neoma knew, just barely managed to survive, with the tenant-farmers scratching a meagre living since the only men they employed were their own sons.

Apart from the fact that she thought it would break her heart for the Manor that had been in the Standish family for over three hundred years to be sold, she thought it likely that they, like Charles, would be unable to find a purchaser.

Peregrine had been watching the expression on her face, and he said:

"You do see that there is nothing else we can do? I reckon that we have exactly a week to get that IOU back into my possession."

"What you have to do," Neoma said firmly, "is go to the Marquis and tell him the truth."

"And leave Charles to find two thousand pounds?" Peregrine asked. "He will have to resign from White's and it is doubtful if any of his friends will speak to him again."

Peregrine's voice dropped for a moment, then he continued angrily:

"I can tell you one thing, Neoma, I am prepared to be a thief and commit every other crime in the calendar, but I would not let down my best friend."

"Yes, dearest ... I do ... understand," she said, "but I am thinking of what Mama would ... say, and how horrified Papa ... would be."

"If Papa had not invested his money so badly," Peregrine replied, "I would not be in the position I am in at this moment."

Neoma had heard him say this before. It still hurt her to hear her father disparaged, even though she had to admit to herself that he had not been very clever where financial matters were concerned.

He was too good-natured, and too interested in his horses and his dogs, to be concerned with the fluctuations of the Financial World, until he realised that his small fortune had almost vanished.

Peregrine leant forward to put his hand on his sister's.

"Please help me, Neoma. You have never failed me yet, and I cannot believe that you would do so now."

The way he spoke and the pleading look in his eyes made Neoma feel that whatever he asked of her she would not refuse.

She had always adored her brother ever since

she was a little girl, and because there was only a year's difference between them, they had been so close that at times she thought they might have been twins.

Because she had always been the practical one, while Peregrine was somewhat reckless and fool-hardy, she had tried ever since the death of her parents to help and guide him—strange though it seemed, since she was the youngest—and to look after and also protect him.

Now she knew that however reprehensible and shocking Peregrine's plan might be, she must either help him or produce an alternative solution to their problem.

Aloud she said:

"You know I will help you, dearest. At the same time, the whole idea . . . horrifies me."

"It horrifies me too," Peregrine said, "but what else can we do? Charles is so ashamed of himself that he would not come round to see you."

"I can understand his feeling like that," Neoma replied, "and perhaps in the future he will drink less. I have thought for some time that both you and Charles were drinking too much."

"Drunk or sober, Charles is almost suicidal now that he realises he could have left the table with about eight thousand pounds in his hands."

"It does not bear thinking about," Neoma replied. "But you cannot really mean that you want me to come with you to stay with the Marquis?"

"I do mean it," Peregrine replied. "You just have to pretend to be like Avril and the other women who will be there."

"If Avril is an actress, how can I pretend to be on the stage when I know nothing about it?" Neoma enquired.

Peregrine looked uncomfortable.

"You do not have to pretend to be on the stage," he said. "You just have to be the sort of woman Avril is."

"I do not . . . understand."

Peregrine rose to walk to the window and stand

looking out at the crab-apple tree. After a moment he said:

"I suppose I could go without you, Neoma, but I do need you, and I have a feeling that somehow you will find the damned IOU if I cannot."

"Do not swear, dearest," Neoma said automatically. "I have told you I will come. It is just that if I have to pretend to be someone other than myself, it is going to be difficult unless you explain to me exactly what I must be like."

"Charles and I are quite certain that no-one will notice you," Peregrine said. "You are there not as my sister but as my 'lady-friend,' and the Marquis is certain to have some woman of his own. His parties, so Charles says, are notorious."

"Notorious for what?" Neoma enquired.

Peregrine did not answer and after a moment she said in a puzzled tone:

"I cannot . . . understand why the Marquis should ask you to bring a woman-friend of your . . . own with you. Surely he knows some ladies he would like to entertain?"

"It is not that kind of party," Peregrine answered in an irritated tone. "Try to understand, Neoma —the female guests will be actresses and woman of that sort. There will be no Chaperones and everyone will be very free and easy."

"I . . . suppose I understand," Neoma said, "but I have a . . . feeling that I will not . . . fit in."

"Of course you will not," Peregrine agreed, "but no-one will realise it except us. You can just keep close to me and say as little as possible. Nobody is going to notice you, especially the Marquis."

"Why do you say it like that?" Neoma asked quickly.

"Because the Marquis is known to patronise the women who are the most notorious 'high-steppers' in London."

Peregrine had not turned round, and Neoma looked at his back with puzzled eyes.

"Do you mean they are . . . famous actresses?"

"That—sort of thing."

"It would be fun to see Maria Foote or Kitty Stephens," Neoma said. "I have often wondered what they are like when they are not on the stage."

She gave a little sigh.

"Not that I have ever been to the Theatre ... although you have promised to take me."

"I will take you if we come back from Syth with the IOU in our pocket."

"Is that the name of the Marquis's house?"

"Of course it is!" Peregrine said. "Really, Neoma, you ought to know that Syth is one of the most important country-houses in England."

"I am sorry, Peregrine, but I have never seen anything about it in the books I have read."

"Well, now you will see it for yourself," Peregrine said. "I believe it is so magnificent that the Regent goes green with envy every time he stays there."

"Then it will be very exciting to see Syth, apart from the fact that I shall feel very out-of-place amongst such grandeur."

She gave a sudden cry.

"What is it?" Peregrine asked, turning round.

"I have just thought," Neoma replied. "Peregrine, how can I possibly go with you? You know I have no smart gowns."

"You look all right as you are," Peregrine said. "As I have already said, nobody is going to notice you, but you might 'doll yourself up' a bit, and of course put on plenty of lip-salve."

Neoma looked at him wide-eyed, then said:

"Is that what actresses do because they wear cosmetics on the stage?"

"Everybody in the *Beau Monde* wears cosmetics," Peregrine said. "Surely you knew that?"

"I never thought about it," Neoma replied. "There has been no need for me to do anything about my face at home. And since I have been in London I have not seen anyone except you and Charles."

"We will buy the sort of things you want," Peregrine said carelessly. "But surely Mama had some? She used to use powder—I know that."

As he spoke, he thought that it was typical of Neoma, whose head was always in the clouds, to have no conception of the Fashionable World or indeed how she should look.

He did not take into account the fact that since their parents' death in a carriage-accident Neoma had lived at the Manor alone except for when he was with her.

When he had brought her to London he had known that there was no money, or at least not enough for both of them to appear in Society, and besides, there was no-one he could ask to chaperone his sister.

Because Peregrine was not entirely selfish, vaguely at the back of his mind he had thought that once he had established himself, he would do what he could for Neoma and find her some friends in London.

But they had only been in the little house in Chelsea for three months and he was still finding his feet, still extremely grateful when he met new friends and was invited to their houses.

It was certainly not the moment to produce a sister—even one who was as attractive as Neoma.

Looking at her now, as if he saw her for the first time, Peregrine told himself that she was attractive—very attractive. In fact, he remembered Charles saying only a month ago:

"You know, Peregrine, Neoma gets prettier all the time. One day she will turn out to be a beauty!"

Peregrine had laughed as if the idea was impossible, but now he was not so sure.

He had seen a number of attractive women since they had come to London, and now he realised that if Neoma was properly dressed and her hair was done in a fashionable manner, she could compare very favourably with them.

"I tell you what, Neoma," he said, "I will give you two guineas, which is all I can afford, to make yourself look smart."

"I will do my best!" Neoma said. "I would not wish to embarrass you."

She took the two guineas from his hand and said:

"You cannot afford it, Peregrine, as I know, and

so I will spend as little as possible. I will buy some
new ribbons to refurbish my gowns, and of course
some lip-salve. Perhaps there was some amongst
Mama's things, but I did not bring many of them to
London."

"We certainly cannot afford to hire a carriage to go
home and look for them," Peregrine replied.

Neoma gave a little sigh.

"If only we could! It would be so lovely to see
the garden again with the lilacs out! The birds will be
nesting in the same bushes and trees as they do every
year. And I am sure the wild deer are missing me."

"They will still be there when we go home,"
Peregrine said briefly. "Do concentrate, Neoma, on being ready by the day after tomorrow."

"Did you say we will be going to the Derby?"

"That is the whole point of the party. Syth is only
ten miles out of London and about five miles from the
Epsom Downs."

"I have always longed to see the Derby," Neoma
said. "And you say that the Marquis is expected to
win it?"

"His horse, Diamond, is the favourite, and as he is
always lucky in everything he touches, he will win it
all right."

"I do not like that envious note in your voice,"
Neoma said. "You know we have always decided between ourselves that we should never be jealous or
envious of anyone. It is a horrid venom which seeps
into the veins and poisons those who feel it."

Peregrine put his arm round his sister.

"It is all very well for you," he said, "but I admit, Neoma, to feeling envious when I see the way other men of my age chuck their money about, and have
plenty to chuck."

"I know it is hard," Neoma said, "but you have
your health and strength and, I think, tucked away
somewhere, a lot of brains!"

Peregrine laughed and pulled her closer.

"You always convince me that things are not as
bad as they seem to be," he said. "But quite frankly,
Neoma, this time we are in a hell of a hole."

"I know, dearest," Neoma said, "and we have to try to get out of it, although for the moment I cannot think of a way."

She paused, then said in a low voice:

"I shall pray ... I shall pray very hard, Peregrine, that there will be an alternative to your and Charles's ... scheme, and perhaps Mama will ... help me to ... find it."

There was silence for a moment, then Peregrine said:

"There is no-one like you, Neoma, and I am grateful. You know that."

"I know, dearest, and we must not despair," Neoma said. "But I admit to feeling a little ... frightened of what we have to do."

As she spoke, she knew that she was frightened, very frightened, but as Peregrine had said—what was the alternative?

She had to help him.

Chapter Two

"How do I look?" Neoma asked as Peregrine came into the room to tell her that the carriage was ready to carry them to Syth.

"All right," he replied without, she thought, even glancing at her.

She was quite used to his paying her no attention, for Peregrine was usually engrossed in his own appearance. But today, because she wanted to look exactly as he wanted her to, she had hoped that he would pay her more heed.

She had scoured the shops near their house for cheap ribbons because those which came from Bond Street were, she was sure, extremely expensive.

She had managed to find two. One was silver, for the evening, and the other was a very pretty pink that she thought made her plain white gown very elegant.

It would have been easier, she thought despairingly, if the fashion had been as it was at the beginning of the century, when every lady, as she had learnt from *The Ladies' Journal,* wore plain white muslin.

Granted, if they were considered to be ultra-smart they wore little or nothing underneath it, so that they often looked extremely indecent, but at the same time Neoma knew that such a fashion could very easily be copied.

She had made all her own gowns since her father's fortune had dwindled away, and she was in fact an experienced seamstress.

"No-one can sew as well as you do, dearest," her mother had said on many occasions.

As it grew more and more difficult to find money to spend on anything but food, Neoma had been glad that she could refurbish her mother's gowns and utilise everything that she could find in the house.

During the war it had been wise when one saw a piece of material to snatch it while one had the chance, and Lady Lionel had bought quite a number of yards of pretty sprigged muslin and those of a more expensive quality which would make into evening-gowns.

Because Neoma wished to look smart when Peregrine was at home, she had made herself two pretty dresses to wear when they had dinner together, and she hoped now, although she rather doubted it, that they would not look hopelessly dowdy at Syth.

She had taken a great deal of trouble to copy sketches which appeared in *The Ladies' Journal,* which usually portrayed only the most elaborate gowns worn at Court Balls or designs which came from Paris.

Nevertheless, because Neoma was imaginative she managed to adapt the outline of them to her own needs, and she thought without conceit that the results were really quite satisfactory.

She had been very undecided as to what she should wear for her arrival at Syth, remembering that her father had always said that first impressions were important.

He was not talking particularly about clothes, but Neoma thought she could not let Peregrine down by letting his friends think the only female he could bring with him was a nondescript country-girl without any touch of London polish.

Accordingly, she trimmed her best day-gown with the pink ribbons and added them to her bonnet, which she knew was not the latest fashion but it was the best she had.

She looked at her reflection in the mirror anxious-

ly and did not, because she was very modest, realise
that in fact she looked very lovely.

Her father had been dark, her mother fair, and
Neoma was a compromise between the two of them.

She thought that her hair was rather nondescript,
but actually it was an unusually soft shade of gold
that in the sunlight had touches of russet red in it.

No-one could look at her without being struck
by the largeness of her eyes and an expression that
was one of transparent purity.

She did not know that her father had once said
to her mother:

"One thing about Neoma is that she could never
lie or be deceitful, for if she ever tried to do anything
so alien to her nature, one would know it immediately just by looking into her eyes."

Her mother had laughed.

"That is true, and I only hope that one day she
will find a man who appreciates such an original quality in a woman."

"She is as sweet and good in her way as you are
in yours," Colonel Standish had answered, and they
had smiled happily at each other.

Neoma had been a pretty child, and although
her brother was not aware of it, she had grown up
into a beauty that made her different in many ways
from the girls who were her contemporaries.

She had small, classical features in an oval
face, but because she was quiet and never self-assertive
it was easy for her to remain unnoticed while other,
more flamboyant beauties caught the eye.

Now, with a faint flush on her cheeks because
she was nervous, and the red salve that Peregrine had
insisted she use to outline the curves of her lips, she
looked very lovely.

It was not surprising that Sir Charles Waddesdon,
coming into the Hall to see what was keeping them,
exclaimed:

"Good Heavens, Neoma! Now that you are all
dressed up, I hardly recognise you."

"Thank you, Charles," Neoma answered, and two
dimples appeared on either side of her mouth.

"I meant it as a compliment," he said quickly.

"You told me exactly what I wanted to hear," Neoma answered. "Has Peregrine told you what name I have chosen?"

"Good Heavens, I had forgotten that!" Charles replied. "For God's sake, Neoma, never let anyone, especially the Marquis, know that you are Peregrine's sister."

He thought that Neoma looked surprised, and he explained:

"He would be censured in no uncertain fashion, I assure you, for taking you to one of His Lordship's disreputable gatherings."

"Peregrine has already told me that I ought ... not to go to ... Syth," Neoma said uncomfortably, "but he insisted I must help him."

"Yes, I know, and it is jolly sporting of you to do so," Charles said. "At the same time, now that I look at you I feel we ought to change our minds."

"Oh, for Heaven's sake, Charles," Peregrine said in an irritated tone, "do not start altering our plans at the last moment. You know as well as I do that I have no-one like Avril whom I can bring with me, and besides, we agreed that we need Neoma's help. She may be able to search for the IOU while you and I keep 'cave.'"

If it had not been so serious, Neoma thought, she would have laughed at the way Peregrine was talking as if they were small boys again on one of their pretended treasure-hunts.

Then she looked at her brother anxiously and said:

"You do ... really want ... me?"

"I have already told you," he answered gruffly, "you have to come! There is no turning back now."

He glared at Charles as he spoke, and his friend said quickly:

"No, of course not, and I am sorry I said what I did. It is just that I was thinking that Neoma is too pretty to be mixed up with the sort of creatures I expect to find at Syth."

"We will look after her," Peregrine said airily,

"and the less she speaks to anyone but us, the better! I have told her to keep out of the way of the Marquis."

"The Marquis will be far too occupied," Charles replied, "but Dadchett will be there, and you know what he is like."

"I have told you already, Neoma," Peregrine said in the tone of a School-Master, "to stick to Charles and me and keep away from all the other men, and if Charles thinks you are looking too pretty, you had better do something about it."

"I am sure no-one will notice me," Neoma said hastily.

"Then come on! Let us get on with it!"

Charles did not move but said to Neoma:

"You were going to tell me what name you have chosen."

"Yes, of course. I thought it ought to be something simple which we could all remember, like King, because we live near the King's Road."

"That is a good idea!" Charles exclaimed. "Neoma King! It sounds quite flashy. And do be careful what you say in front of Avril, for she is a terrible gossip!"

This remark did not make Neoma feel any more confident, but Peregrine was already carrying her small trunk outside to where the carriage was waiting.

They had had a long argument about what sort of conveyance they should hire to take them to Syth, and Peregrine had of course favoured riding in style in a Phaeton.

But Phaetons held only two people comfortably, and to hire two would have been an unwarranted expenditure.

What was more, Avril had told Charles that she had no intention of arriving with her hair blown about, or bedraggled if there was a shower of rain.

They had therefore decided on a closed travelling-carriage in which the two girls would sit on the back-seat, with Peregrine and Charles facing them.

"If there is one thing I really dislike, it is being

couped up in a vehicle and not being able to see where I am going!" Peregrine had complained.

"You can hardly sit on the box with the coachman," Charles had replied, "although we might arrive in better style if you pretended to be a footman!"

Peregrine had thrown a cushion at him for such impertinence, and it had taken some time for them to settle down again and go on trying to decide the momentous question of the manner of their arrival.

In fact, everything that was said about Syth made Neoma more nervous and more uncomfortable about the part she had to play.

There was no doubt that her mother would have been horrified at her staying in a house-party with women whom she knew they would not have entertained at home.

Mrs. Standish had always spoken of actresses as being inferior creatures with whom she, and certainly all of her friends, would not deign to associate.

Although Neoma had no idea of what Peregrine had meant when he had added: "those sort of women," she felt that they were questionable and she grew more and more worried about the part she was expected to play.

Although it would be exciting to be at Syth and certainly to escape if only for a little while from the lonely existence she spent in their house in Royal Avenue, she wished that she could be a guest under less difficult circumstances.

She had lain awake at night worrying about how it could be possible to find in a big house the IOU with Peregrine's signature on it, for they had not the slightest idea where the Marquis kept such things.

But when she expressed her fears to Peregrine he merely replied:

"Do not worry. We will just have to see what we can discover when we are there. Most men keep such things in their desk or perhaps in a drawer in their bedroom."

"You cannot possibly expect me to go into the Marquis's bedroom?" Neoma asked.

"You are certainly not to do that!" Peregrine replied. "Charles or I will have a look. We will just have to use our brains and think of ourselves as being Detectives like the Bow Street Runners."

Neoma thought with a little sigh that it was becoming like one of their pretend games, and she was quite certain in her own mind that they would come away from Syth just as empty-handed as when they had arrived.

But it was no use saying so, and whatever happened, she was committed to helping Peregrine because he relied on her.

When he had heaved her trunk up onto the box beside the driver and opened the door of the carriage, Neoma stepped in, knowing that Avril was waiting inside.

She had a glimpse of a high-brimmed bonnet covered with emerald-green ostrich-feathers, and then a hand was outstretched towards her and a voice which was warm and friendly but definitely uncultured said:

"'Allo! I began to think you wasn't coming!"

"I am sorry to have kept you waiting," Neoma replied, sitting down on the seat.

As she did so, she thought that Avril was certainly very pretty but flamboyant beyond anything she had expected.

She had dark hair, flashing dark eyes fringed with long, mascaraed eye-lashes, and crimson lips, and she was wearing an emerald-green silk gown which revealed every curve of her figure and showed to advantage the diamond necklace which matched the glittering diamonds in her ears.

"I say—this is going to be fun!" she said to Neoma. "I couldn't believe me ears when Charles told me we'd been invited to Syth."

She gave a little laugh and said:

"I never thought the 'Imperious Marquis' would get round to asking little Avril to stay!"

"The 'Imperious Marquis'?" Peregrine repeated. "That is a very good name for him."

"That's what the girls at the Theatre calls him, because he's so stiff-necked," Avril answered. "He comes round to see *Madame* Vestris sometimes, and looks at all of us like we was dirt beneath his feet!"

"That is how he treats us as well!" Charles said, laughing.

"Well, anyone can 'ave him for all I care," Avril said. "Give me m' old Nob from the North. He may be a bit of an old bore, but at least he's jolly when he's had some champagne, and ever so generous—when he gets what he wants!"

She gave a sudden cry and exclaimed:

"You kicked me and it hurt!"

"I am sorry," Charles answered, but he looked at Peregrine as he spoke, and Peregrine said hastily to Neoma:

"I hope you have brought a sunshade with you. It will be very hot driving to the Derby tomorrow."

"I remembered," Neoma said with a smile. "I thought we would be going to the race-course in open carriages."

"No, in a coach," Peregrine replied. "They say it is half the fun to be in a coach at the Derby, but the roads are terribly crowded."

"I remember when I went last year," Charles said. "There were a great many accidents."

"I hope we won't be involved in one!" Avril cried. "One of the chorus was thrown out of a Phaeton when the horses bolted, and she had her leg broke!"

"How terrible!" Neoma said. "What happened to her?"

"She lost her part," Avril said carelessly, "and I don't suppose she had much saved."

"What did she do?" Neoma enquired.

"Luckily her 'friend' coughed up, though he wasn't very keen when she was no use to him."

Neoma thought that the friend in question must have something to do with the Theatre, but Charles began to talk very animatedly about something different and she was unable to ask any more questions.

It was quite an amusing drive because Peregrine and Charles were in good spirits and vied with each other in entertaining Avril.

Neoma had the idea, although she could not un-

derstand why, that they did not wish to give the pretty
actress much chance of talking, but anyway the time
passed very pleasantly until Charles suddenly exclaimed:

"Here are the gates! We are here!"

"Oh, Heavens, why didn't you tell me before?"
Avril exclaimed, and drew from her reticule a small
mirror.

She tidied her hair under her bonnet, then took a
pot of salve and applied it thickly to her lips, making
them redder than they had been before and rather
vulgar, Neoma decided, although she repressed the
thought.

She was not concerned with Avril, however, but
with her first glimpse of Syth.

She had not missed the enormous gold-tipped
wrought-iron gates surmounted by a coronet and
flanked on either side by two extremely attractive
lodges.

They moved down a drive of ancient oak-trees,
then descended into a valley, and by craning her neck
almost out of the open window Neoma could see just
ahead of them a lake, and on the other side of it, silhouetted against a background of trees, the most magnificent house she had ever seen.

She had taken the trouble, even in the short time
available, to persuade Charles to tell her a little about
Syth.

He knew far more about buildings than did Peregrine, and although he had never been to Syth, he
knew that it had been designed by John Vanburgh
and his co-adjutor, Nicholas Hawksmoor.

Because her mother had taught Neoma a great
deal about architecture, she knew that these two men
were responsible for building Blenheim Palace, which
had been given by the nation to the victorious Duke
of Marlborough, and also for the great domes of St.
Paul's Cathedral and for Greenwich Hospital.

She therefore expected Syth to be impressive, but
when at last she could see it her breath was taken
away.

Never had she imagined that a private house could be so magnificent.

Not surprisingly, the centre block was surmounted by a dome and the whole house winged out almost interminably.

It was so impressive that Neoma drew in her breath and thought that she was dreaming and it could not in fact be real.

The horses drew them nearer and they passed over a bridge which spanned the lake, then there was a huge courtyard and an entrance which might have belonged to a King's Palace.

Even Avril was impressed.

"Cor!" she exclaimed. "Fancy living in a place like this! No wonder the Marquis thinks himself imperious! But at least he's got something to be stiff-necked about!"

"Do be careful what you say, Avril!" Charles admonished. "We do not want to be thrown out before we have been to the Derby."

"I'll be ever so sweet to him," Avril promised, "and if you get jealous, don't blame me!"

She gave him a provocative glance from under her blackened eye-lashes, and Charles smiled at her in an intimate manner which made Neoma feel slightly embarrassed.

Peregrine was concerned with more important things.

"Have you enough money to pay for the carriage?" he asked Charles.

"Leave it to me," Charles replied. "I managed to cash a post-dated cheque, and if we do not lose money at the races I have enough for the whole visit."

"Lose money?" Neoma repeated with a little cry. "Neither of you are to bet!"

Even as she spoke, she realised that such a statement was out of keeping with the part she was supposed to be playing, and Avril looked surprised. Then she said:

" 'Ere! You keep tabs on Peregrine's money and leave Charles to me! I know he hasn't got much, but what he's got is mine, and I'll tell you why when we're alone!"

"I hope you will do nothing of the sort!" Charles said quickly. "Neoma does not want to hear the intimate details of your life."

"Why not? It's no secret that his Nibs doesn't part easily with cash."

At that moment the carriage came to a standstill beside the steps which led up to the front door, and Neoma forgot what Avril was saying in her interest in watching half-a-dozen footmen in resplendent livery appear on the steps, one of whom opened the carriage-door.

Then there was a red carpet on which to walk, and Neoma was glad that Avril flounced ahead of her, her silk gown rustling and the feathers seeming to float on her bonnet.

Standing up, she was very much shorter than Neoma had expected, and it struck her that she was in fact rather like a small parakeet, colourful and proud of her plumage, despite the fact that her surroundings were so awesome.

The Hall was certainly in keeping with the exterior of the house, with a huge double staircase sweeping up to the next floor, the walls covered with fine pictures, and beneath the stairs some exquisite statues set on marble plinths.

But there was no time to do anything but follow a resplendent Major Domo who led them along a wide corridor where there were more statues, pictures, and furniture which made Neoma long to stop and examine them.

She was well aware that both Charles and Peregrine, behind her, were awed into silence.

They walked for what seemed to be an immeasurably long way before a door was opened and they were shown into an enormous room which was even more resplendent than that part of the house which they had seen already.

Neoma had a quick glimpse of velvet-upholstered sofas and chairs with gold frames, a number of long windows where the curtains were surmounted by gold pelmets, and a marble mantelpiece carved in stone.

Then she had eyes only for the man who was standing talking to several gentlemen who were as elegant as Peregrine and Charles and three women who were as colourful and gaudy as Avril.

There was no need for anyone to tell her that this was the Marquis of Rosyth, for he appeared to dominate not only his guests but the immense room itself.

Never had she imagined that a man could look so distinguished. Although he was tall, he seemed, because of the way he held himself and the vibrations emanating from him, to be even taller than he actually was.

But what was even more arresting about the Marquis was the expression on his face.

It was obvious why Avril had called him the Imperious Marquis, for his expression was one of cynicism and disdain, as if everybody were beneath his condescension.

He was still young, and yet the lines on his face might have been those of an older man, and his eyes, Neoma thought, were as hard as agates.

The Major Domo had asked Peregrine and Charles their names, and Neoma thought it strange that while the gentlemen were announced, she and Avril remained anonymous.

"Sir Charles Waddesdon and Mr. Peregrine Standish, My Lord!"

The two names seemed lost in the big room, and Neoma felt as if she herself had suddenly shrunk to the point where she was almost too insignificant even to be seen.

The Marquis held out his hand to Charles.

"I am glad to see you, Waddesdon! And you, Standish!"

"May I introduce Miss Avril Lisle, My Lord," Charles said, "who is appearing in *The Beggars' Opera.*"

"I must have seen you," the Marquis said to Avril.

"If you don't remember me, I well remember you!" she challenged.

"I shall remember another time," the Marquis said.

But Neoma thought he spoke not as if he was paying her a compliment but merely throwing a coin to an importunate beggar.

"Have you heard the marriage-story about your friend *Madame* Vestris, My Lord?" Avril asked, as if determined to hold her host's attention.

"I expect so," he replied, "but tell me."

"When *Madame* was about to be married, we were told that before accepting Mr. Vestris she made him a full confession of all her lovers."

Avril looked at the Marquis provocatively under her eye-lashes as she finished:

"Her understudy exclaimed: 'What a *wonderful* memory!' "

Those standing beside the Marquis laughed uproariously, but he turned from Avril to Neoma, and Peregrine said hastily:

"Miss King, My Lord!"

Neoma curtseyed and just for a moment her hand touched the Marquis's.

She thought his fingers were cold—as cold, she told herself, as he seemed to be towards his guests, and she wondered why he bothered to invite them.

"Are you on the stage, Miss King?" he enquired.

"No, My Lord."

He looked from her to Peregrine and she had the feeling that something surprised him, although she could not think what it could be.

The two men were then introduced to the other guests in the party, and a servant appeared with a silver tray on which there were glasses of champagne, and then everyone seemed to be talking at once.

Neoma took a glass because she felt that it was expected of her, but it was in fact a very long time since she had tasted champagne, and then only a sip at Christmas when her father had asked her to join him in drinking her mother's health.

She was afraid that she might find it intoxicating

and she therefore drank only a very little, seeing with surprise that the other women gulped it down and their glasses were immediately refilled by one of the footmen.

There were more arrivals, and as Peregrine seemed to be immersed in a conversation, with one of the men-guests on the merits of the horses that were running tomorrow, Neoma managed to edge herself a little way from the group.

She wanted to look round her at the pictures on the walls and the furniture which stood beneath them.

They were all so superlative that she told herself that whatever else happened at this party, she must seize the opportunity to see everything she could and remember it afterwards.

She wished above all things that her mother was with her, because Mrs. Standish would not only have been thrilled by such treasures but would have known the history of them.

'There must be somebody in the house who can tell me what I want to know!' Neoma thought.

She was so intent on what she was seeing that she heard nothing that was said by the other guests until she realised that everyone was being escorted by the Marquis to the Hall.

"My Housekeeper will show you to your rooms," he said.

Trailing behind Avril, Neoma walked up the staircase, realising that it was of gilt and in a beautiful and elaborate design which she was certain was French.

Again they walked for a long way along wide corridors, and now the Housekeeper, rustling along in a black dress with a silver chatelaine swinging from her waist, was leading the procession of ladies, while the gentlemen had been left to the Groom of the Chambers.

"You are here, Miss," the Housekeeper said finally to Neoma, and she found herself in one of the prettiest rooms she had ever seen.

The walls were pink and so were the hangings of the bed, which fell from a small carved dome surmounted by a coronet.

"How lovely!" Neoma exclaimed. "It is the prettiest bed I have ever seen!"

"This is known as 'Queen of Scots Room,'" the Housekeeper explained, "because Mary Queen of Scots once slept here."

"How interesting!" Neoma said. "I hope I shall dream of her when I sleep in it."

"I daresay you'll have other things to dream about, Miss," the Housekeeper said in what Neoma thought was a disapprovingly frigid tone.

The woman walked across the room as she spoke and opened a door by the fireplace.

"The gentleman who accompanied you is in the next room, Miss," she went on, "and this is the communicating-door."

Neoma was just about to say how glad she was that Peregrine was near her, but she remembered that he was not supposed to be her brother and she thought the Housekeeper might think it a strange remark.

Instead, she looked to where two young housemaids were unpacking her trunk and hanging up her gowns in a wardrobe.

"Could you tell me what time dinner will be served?" she asked.

"The guests are expected downstairs in the French Salon in three-quarters-of-an-hour, Miss," the Housekeeper replied, "and His Lordship dislikes it if anyone is late."

"I will not be late!" Neoma said quickly. "That would be extremely bad manners."

She spoke impulsively, and she thought for a moment that the Housekeeper seemed to relax a little.

"One of the maids will assist you to dress, Miss, and your bath is ready in the small dressing-room next door."

"How very luxurious!" Neoma said. "I have never seen such a magnificent house or so many treasures!"

She gave the Housekeeper a nervous glance and added:

"If you have a moment while I am here, perhaps you could tell me a little of the history of Syth and of the things in it."

The Housekeeper looked surprised.

"I'm pleased you are interested, Miss," she said. "You will find that Mr. Greystone, the Curator, will be willing to tell you everything you want to know."

"That will be wonderful!" Neoma exclaimed. "How can I find him?"

"Mr. Greystone has an office in the East Wing," the Housekeeper said. "If you ask one of the footmen, he will take you to him."

"Thank you. Thank you very much for telling me."

Again she thought the Housekeeper looked surprised at the eagerness of her tone. Then, afraid that if she lingered she might be late for dinner, Neoma began to take off her bonnet.

As she bathed and dressed she was wondering if she would have to find her own way to the French Salon, when there came a knock on the communicating-door, and when she called: "Come in!" Peregrine appeared.

"I was so hoping that you would come," she said. "I did not want to go down alone."

"No, of course not. We will go together," Peregrine replied.

As the maid who had helped her dress was about to leave the room tactfully, Neoma said quickly:

"Thank you very much for helping me. It was very kind of you."

The maid withdrew and she said to Peregrine:

"Have you ever seen a more fantastic house? I do wish Mama were here! Think how she would have enjoyed the pictures, and just look at my bed!"

"Do be careful what you say," Peregrine warned her, looking over his shoulder. "No-one would expect to hear you talking to me about your mother."

"I cannot see why not," Neoma replied for the sake of argument. "After all, you might have known me for years and met my mother when you called."

"Oh, for Heaven's sake, Neoma," Peregrine said crossly, "we are not supposed to know each other all that well."

Neoma thought of Avril and said:

"I was only teasing, dearest. I think frankly that Mama would have been rather shocked by the appearance of the other women staying here."

"Of course she would have been," Peregrine agreed, "and I have said a hundred times already that you ought not to be here either, but you promised to help me."

"Which I have every intention of doing," Neoma replied. "But do you imagine for one moment that we shall find what we are looking for in this enormous house? It will be like looking for a needle in a haystack!"

"We shall just have to wait and see," Peregrine said.

But she had the feeling that his hope of obtaining what he wanted was ebbing away.

They went down the stairs side-by-side, Neoma craning her neck to look up at the painted ceiling which was a riot of gods and goddesses.

She was even more impressed by the French Salon.

She recognised the furniture as being Louis XIV, and some of the pieces were Buhl, while the rest were carved and gilded.

But it was the pictures that kept Neoma looking and looking again. She found it difficult to concentrate on the other guests, who were chattering, she thought, exactly like the parakeets they reminded her of, in their elaborate gowns.

The women seemed to out-vie one another not only in brilliant colours but in wearing a profusion of jewellery, a great deal of which Neoma suspected was not real.

But they shimmered and glittered and the egrets in their hair seemed to move mystically so that she wondered if they were a mirage which had no reality.

Then the Marquis came into the room and everything seemed to become very real indeed.

He had looked impressive in his day-clothes, but dressed for the evening he seemed to overpower everybody so that they shrank beside him.

The women obviously wished to ingratiate themselves with him, and they left the gentlemen with whom they had been talking and ran towards him with little excited cries of pleasure, fluttering their darkened eyelashes and pouting their crimson lips in an obvious effort to attract his attention.

Peregrine was talking to somebody else and Neoma found herself standing alone.

As she looked at the Marquis it seemed as if he suddenly saw her isolated and making no effort to join those who thronged round him.

As he looked over their heads, Neoma felt as if their eyes met and she was sure that he was critical of her appearance.

Not knowing what to do, she looked hastily for Peregrine, then moved to his side.

"Are there any other horses you fancy in the Derby apart from *Diamond*, My Lord?" she heard Peregrine ask the gentleman to whom he was speaking.

Neoma realised that instead of answering, the gentleman was looking at her. He looked about forty and she had the impression, from the lines under his eyes, that he was somewhat debauched.

"Introduce me, my boy," he said to Peregrine.

Because she knew her brother so well, she was aware that Peregrine was reluctant to do anything of the sort.

But the gentleman was obviously waiting, and after a moment Peregrine said:

"May I present Lord Dadchett—Miss King!"

Lord Dadchett put out his hand and held Neoma's as she dropped him a curtsey.

"I am delighted, very delighted to meet you, Miss King! I have the idea that you have never stayed in such a large and interesting house as this before."

"No, My Lord."

"Then as I know it well, I am sure I can show you things that will interest you."

There was something in the way he spoke which gave Neoma a warning of danger.

She was also aware that Peregrine was fidgeting beside her.

"That is very kind of you, My Lord," she replied, "but Mr. Standish has already promised to be
my guide."

As she spoke she saw Lord Dadchett's eyes narrow, and she had the feeling that he would not be put
off or disconcerted by her refusal.

"That is the right answer, Miss King," he said,
"but let me tell you I am not easily circumvented
from doing what I particularly wish to do."

As he spoke he walked away, and Neoma looked
at Peregrine.

She was half-afraid that he would be annoyed
with her for having refused Lord Dadchett's suggestion, but instead he said in a low voice which could
not be overheard:

"Keep away from that man—have nothing to do
with him, I warn you!"

"Yes, of course," Neoma agreed.

*   *   *

The Marquis, with a lady on his arm, was leading the way from the Salon and now everyone began
to follow him, each gentleman escorting a lady, the
ones, Neoma suspected, whom they had brought with
them.

Avril, resplendent in a ruby-red gown which
Neoma thought had a remarkably low décolletage,
was holding on to Charles's hand and talking to him
in a surprisingly intimate manner.

Peregrine offered her his arm and she slipped
her hand into it. Because she thought he was still upset
by Lord Dadchett, she said in a voice that only he
could hear:

"Do not worry, Peregrine. Whatever else happens,
I shall always be thrilled that I have come here and
seen this magnificent, marvellous house! It is far more
exciting to me even than the Derby!"

Peregrine laughed and it was quite spontaneous.

"Do not let anyone else hear you say that," he
admonished. "The men are talking of nothing but the
racing."

"You will not be betting?" Neoma asked.

"What with?" Peregrine asked bitterly. "Why cannot I have a house like this and a horse like *Diamond?*"

Because he obviously felt so strongly about it and because in a way it was so absurd, Neoma laughed.

"For the same reason," she said, "that I cannot be the Queen of Sheba!"

It was the sort of retort they had made to each other ever since they were children, and quite suddenly they began to giggle.

"The joke is," Peregrine said in her ear, "that we have no right to be here, you especially, but nobody else realises it!"

"I hope not!"

As Neoma spoke, she realised that they had reached the Dining-Room table and a flunkey was showing them where they were to sit

As she sat down, she looked over the profusion of gold plate to where at the head of the table the Marquis of Rosyth, in a high-backed chair, looked like a King.

Again her eyes met his and she had the uncomfortable feeling that while everybody else accepted her for what she appeared to be, the Marquis was aware of her pretence. Then she told herself that she was being absurd.

Why, with so many other attractive women present, should he be interested in her?

Because she was nervous, she forced herself to look critically at those who sat on either side of him.

The appearance of the woman on his right, whom he had escorted to dinner, convinced her that any idea that the Marquis had given her even so much as a passing glance was ridiculous.

Never had she seen anyone so alluring, so seductive.

If Avril had seemed over-dressed when Neoma had met her in the carriage, she now realized, starting with the lady on the Marquis's right, that everyone with the exception of herself was now extremely under-dressed.

Never had she imagined that women could wear

such low décolletages without being completely naked, and when they bent forward at the table Neoma found herself blushing.

As for the woman on the Marquis's right, she understood now what Peregrine had meant by a "high-stepper."

Her eyes slanted mysteriously, her lips curved provocatively, and her red hair flamed like a banner of fire.

There was a necklace of huge emeralds round her neck, which Neoma was certain was real, and because she was so interested she said to Peregrine:

"Who is that sitting beside the Marquis?"

"Vicky Vale," he replied, as if she was expected to know who he meant. "She is called 'La Flame'!"

"The Flame?" Neoma translated. "Why?"

There was silence as Peregrine obviously sought an explanation. Then he said:

"I expect it became her nickname after she had acted in some particular part."

"She is an actress?"

"Not exactly—I mean not at the moment."

"She is amazing!" Neoma ejaculated. "I have never seen anyone like her!"

"I do not suppose there is anyone like her," Peregrine replied, "and certainly only someone like the Marquis could afford her!"

The words seemed to slip out, and he added quickly:

"I mean, of course, afford to—entertain her. She expects to be made a tremendous fuss of, as you can imagine."

"Yes, of course," Neoma said.

She felt that his explanation did not ring true but was just thought up on the spur of the moment.

She could understand the Marquis wishing to dine with anyone so alluring, but why, she wondered, should he bother to entertain the other women who sat round the table?

The gentlemen were all obviously well-bred, but the women not only spoke in the same common voices as Avril, but they looked both vulgar and gaudy.

'I suppose because they are actresses they are amusing,' Neoma thought to herself.

She tried to listen to what they said, but they did not appear to be saying anything very witty but were only flirting, if that was the right word, with the men on either side of them.

They also seemed to be lifting their glasses to their lips in toasts to one another and to their dinner-partners.

They even drank out of the men's glasses, or made them drink out of theirs, which seemed to Neoma very strange indeed.

The food that was served was delicious and she appreciated the fact that it was all on gold dishes which bore the Marquis's crest.

Neoma had never eaten off gold plate before and she found it difficult not to let her knife and fork squeak.

She realised that while she was successful in eating delicately, some of the other women were not only noisy but were upsetting their food down the fronts of their gowns.

It seemed to her extraordinary until with a sudden shock she realised halfway through the meal that a great number of the ladies had obviously had too much to drink.

She imagined that the men had too, but they had more control over their behaviour.

But their faces seemed to get red and their cravats began to crease and wilt round their chins.

As time passed the women appeared, in Neoma's eyes, to get more vulgar every moment.

Their hair was loosened and they seemed continually to be having trouble in keeping their gowns from falling even lower than they were already. A woman opposite her knocked over a glass of claret, which flowed over the table and had to be mopped up by an attendant.

As the Dining-Room table looked so fine with its chased gold ornaments and elegant arrangement of green orchids, Neoma felt that the behaviour of the guests jarred on the scene.

Again she wondered why the Marquis should wish to entertain such people.

There were so many things she wanted to ask Peregrine, but she was afraid that they might be overheard.

She also had the uncomfortable feeling that he too was having too much to drink.

After she had refused any more wine and the crystal glasses at her side had been left untouched, one of the servants asked:

"Would you like some lemonade, Miss?"

"Yes, please," Neoma said gratefully, and when the lemonade was poured out for her, she drank it thirstily.

For the first time during the evening the gentleman on her other side turned to her and asked:

"Do my eyes deceive me, or is that lemonade you are drinking?"

"It is lemonade!" Neoma said with a smile.

"Good God!" the gentleman replied. "I never thought I would sit at this table and find one of the Marquis's guests drinking lemonade. We will have Grace and Psalm-singing before we have finished!"

There was so much disgust in his voice that Neoma gave a little peal of laughter.

"I am sorry if it upsets you," she said, "but I think quite a number of people here would do well to ask for some lemonade rather than drink any more wine."

The gentleman turned round in his seat to look at her.

"Who are you?" he asked. "You sound like one of those damned reformers who are always petitioning me in the House of Commons. I send them away with a flea in their ear—I can tell you that!"

He spoke in an aggressive manner and because Neoma was interested she asked:

"You are a Member of Parliament?"

"I am!"

"How interesting! Which Constituency do you represent?"

"One on the South Coast," he replied. "But I

have not come here to talk Politics but to enjoy myself."

"And do you not enjoy your Politics?"

He looked at her for a moment.

"Look here!" he said. "I know what you are! You are a spoil-sport! I want to enjoy myself and I want to drink. Is that clear?"

"Very clear!" Neoma answered, rather disconcerted.

She found that she was talking to the gentleman's back, for he had turned round to give his attention to the woman on his other side.

'This is a very strange party,' she thought to herself.

She was to repeat that thought with increasing dismay as the party grew stranger and stranger.

The servants extinguished all the lights except for the candelabra on the table, then left the room.

Then it seemed that everybody became abandoned in a manner that Neoma found shocking and even disgusting.

The gentlemen were kissing the women next to them, and it was quite obvious that some of them were behaving in a manner which made her look away and deliberately not look in their direction again.

Only one person seemed unchanged since the meal had begun and that was the Marquis.

He was sitting back in his high chair at the top of the table, while Vicky Vale was whispering in his ear and doing everything to hold his attention and keep his interest.

As she watched him, Neoma saw that he was in fact surveying his guests with a faintly mocking smile on his lips, as if he was cynically amused at their abandonment and their loss of dignity.

Not for one second did he relinquish his, and it suddenly struck Neoma that he was like a male Circe, the enchantress who by her magic powers had turned her guests into swine.

'Why does he do this? Why does he behave in such a strange way?' she wondered.

She felt that Peregrine would become spellbound

by the Marquis and dragged down into depths of depravity that she could not even imagine.

'We should not be here!' she thought frantically. 'This is evil!'

Chapter Three

Neoma awoke and thought that the party last night had been a nightmare and she had dreamt it.

Then she knew it had been real and thought once again that she must somehow get Peregrine away from Syth.

She had never, in her innocence, imagined that anything could be so degrading as the dinner-party had been.

She had, because she read a great deal, found in some of her books mentions of orgies given by Roman noblemen and of Bacchanalian feasts held in honour of Bacchus.

But no details had been given of what actually occurred and they had therefore meant nothing real to Neoma.

Last night, however, had indeed been real and she had sat feeling first surprised, then deeply shocked until her whole body was tense.

She tried to speak to Peregrine but he would not listen to her, and she finally realised that he had had so much to drink that whatever she said, he would not understand.

Because she could not bear to see men and women degrading themselves in such an undignified way, she ceased to look round the table and instead stared at the orchids, trying to pretend that she was alone and this was not happening.

It was difficult, however, not to be aware of the

drunken laughter and of the occasional shrieks from the women, above the clatter of glasses, that rose higher and higher.

It was then that she heard a woman, who was sitting a little way down the table beside the local Member of Parliament, say in a loud voice:

"I want to go to the ordinary!"

For a moment Neoma felt that she could not have heard her aright.

She could not imagine any woman could speak so indecently or so indelicately in front of a gentleman, but as the woman rose from her seat and moved somewhat unsteadily towards the door, she knew that this was her opportunity.

"I am going to bed," she whispered to Peregrine, but she was sure he did not hear her.

Then she hurried from the room, and when she was outside in the corridor, without thinking of anything but a desire to escape, she ran into the Hall and up the stairs.

When she reached her own bedroom she locked the door and stood against it almost as if she was afraid of being pursued.

The maid who had helped her dress had told her to ring when she retired if she wanted help in undoing her gown.

Neoma felt that she could see no-one and speak to no-one. She only wanted to be alone, and somehow to expunge from her mind what she had seen and heard downstairs.

She undressed slowly, and then as she said her prayers she cried out to her mother to help her, to come to her and to show her how to save Peregrine.

"He is too young, Mama," she pleaded, "and he is impressed by the Marquis and his friends and he will think that is the way gentlemen should behave, but I am sure Papa was never like that . . . never, never!"

As she crept into bed, she thought at first that it would be impossible to sleep, that she would be haunted by pictures of half-naked women and the way they were kissing and being fondled by the drunken gentlemen.

But because she was very tired and had sat up half the night before, pressing and retrimming her gowns, she had fallen into a deep, dreamless slumber and mercifully knew no more. . . .

Now Neoma realised that it was very early and there was pale sunshine showing between the curtains as she rose from the bed to walk across the room to one of the windows.

She pulled back the curtains and looked out.

Whatever horrors might lie inside Syth, outside it was exceedingly beautiful.

The sun turned the lake into a mirror of pale gold and she could see swans moving majestically over the surface of it.

Under the trees in the Park were spotted deer such as she had loved at home, only here there were many more of them.

The green lawns, the flower-beds, and the shrubs sloping down to the lake were a riot of colour.

Neoma looked at the clock and saw that it was only a few minutes after half-past-five.

An idea came to her and she looked again at the beauty outside.

She knew that they were not leaving for the races until noon, and she was quite certain that the guests in the house-party would be too tired or perhaps too ill after their indulgence of the night before to be ready until the last moment.

She wondered how Peregrine was.

There was no doubt that he would feel ill, for he always did when he drank too much, and she hated the Marquis for encouraging Peregrine and Charles into making pigs of themselves.

'I am right in thinking that he turns his guests into swine!' Neoma thought. 'But why? Why should that please him?'

She had known that with the exception of herself, he had been the only person at the table in complete control of his behaviour.

She suspected, although she had no evidence of it, that he had drunk very little but had just watched the debauchery round him as if he were at a play.

"It is horrible and cruel!" Neoma told herself, thinking again of Peregrine with a constriction of her heart.

She washed and dressed herself, taking very little trouble over the arrangement of her hair and forgetting, in her eagerness to be out in the fresh air, to use any cosmetics.

Then she thought that she must just see if Peregrine was all right, and very softly she opened the communicating-door.

She had thought when she went to bed that she would hear him when he retired, but she found that there were two doors, one against the other, and when she opened the one into Peregrine's room she heard him snoring and knew that he was still infected by the fumes of alcohol.

Peregrine never snored unless he had had too much to drink.

The curtains were drawn and it took Neoma a moment to adjust her eyes to the darkness. Then she saw that Peregrine had not rung for a valet to assist him to bed, obviously not being in a state to remember to do so.

Instead he had flung his evening-coat down on the floor, pulled off his shoes, and then just flopped down on the bed as he was.

Neoma moved nearer to him and even in the dim light in the bedroom she could see how pale he looked and that there were dark lines under his eyes.

The cravat round his neck was a crumpled wreck, his evening-shirt, which she had washed and pressed with such care, was stained with port, and there were also marks on his evening-trousers.

Neoma gave a little sigh.

She would have liked to take away his shirt and soak it, hoping that the stains were erasable and he would not have to buy another one, but she knew that she must not disturb him.

She thought too, as she stood looking down at him, how young and vulnerable he was.

'I must talk to him about leaving,' she thought to

herself, but she knew it would have to wait until he would listen to her sensibly.

She bent down to pick up his evening-coat and hang it on the back of a chair, then crept from the room, shutting the communicating-doors very quietly behind her.

Because she was certain that no-one would see her, she did not bother to wear a bonnet.

At home she had always walked about bareheaded, and she wanted now to feel the freshness of the air. She even hoped that there was a wind that would blow away some of her apprehension and anxiety.

She walked quickly down the corridor, realising that someone had extinguished the candles which the night before had been burning in silver sconces.

As she reached the top of the stairs, she saw that the doors in the Hall were open.

She remembered that her mother had told her that in big houses the servants rose very early. She was therefore not surprised when she saw footmen in their shirt-sleeves carrying trays of glasses, maids in mob-caps brushing the carpets, and others carrying pails of water out onto the steps.

They looked at Neoma in surprise as she passed them, but answered politely as she wished them good-morning.

Then she was out in the fresh air and she felt for the moment as if she had escaped from a trap that had imprisoned her.

She thought at first that she would walk down to the lake. Then it struck her that she might be seen from the windows and somebody, maybe even the Marquis himself, would think it strange that she was up so early.

Instead, she looked at the West Wing of the house and was certain that beyond it were buildings which she suspected were the stables.

She had visited, with her father, several large houses near their home, where the stables had not been far from the main building, and these visits always ended with an inspection of their host's horses.

Neoma moved round the corner of the West Wing and there, sure enough, she found a large archway built of the same stone as the house and surmounted by the Marquis's coat-of-arms.

Through it she could see two long buildings on either side of a cobbled yard, and dozens of horses' heads protruding from the half-open doors.

This, to Neoma, was almost as exciting as the pictures in the house.

She had ridden almost before she could walk and had vied with Peregrine as to who was the more proficient horseman.

She was only nine when she first went out hunting with her father, and because she was completely fearless she soon dispensed with her pony, helped him to exercise his own horses, and often rode them out hunting.

She was invariably one of the first in the field, and although her mother protested that such long days were too much for her, her father encouraged her, saying that she rode as well as he did, and he had no higher praise to offer.

First because she loved her horses, and then because when they had less money they were always short-handed in the stables, Neoma herself had looked after the horses she rode and others as well.

They had meant more to her than her friends, and it was the love she gave them that made even the most difficult horses amenable when she rode them.

Slowly now she moved along the open stables, patting the horses' necks, talking to them, and knowing that she had never seen a collection of finer or better-bred animals.

If the Marquis's race-horses were as good as these, it was not surprising that he was expected to win the Derby.

She had almost finished one side of the stables when she heard voices and realised that they came from the next stall.

She looked through the half-open door and saw an elderly groom with a poultice in his hand.

"Now 'old 'im steady," he was saying to a stable-lad who had the horse by the bridle.

This was obviously easier said than done, for the horse, afraid of the poultice, or perhaps from sheer devilment, was bucking and kicking and neighing indignantly.

"Oi can't hold 'im, Mr. Hewson—Oi can't!" the stable-lad cried.

As he spoke, he let the horse's bridle go and scuttled from the back of the stall to the front.

He was very pale, there were beads of sweat on his forehead, and he was breathing heavily, which told Neoma that he was in fact frightened.

She opened the stable-door, saying to the groom as she did so:

"Perhaps I can help."

The old groom looked at her in astonishment.

"Ye can't do that, Ma'am! Ye mustn't come in 'ere! This 'orse be dangerous!"

"I am not afraid," Neoma said, "and I am sure I can manage him."

She walked forward as she spoke. The groom put out his hands as if to stop her, then realised that he was holding the hot poultice.

"No, Ma'am, stop, Ma'am!" he cried, but Neoma paid no attention.

She talked quietly in the tone she had always used to her own horses.

Then she walked to the end of the stall and stood with her back to the manger.

"What is the matter, boy?" she asked. "Have they upset you? We have to make you well. It will only hurt for a minute, then it will soon be better, and think how pleased you will be with yourself."

At first the horse only put back his ears and let out a defiant kick in the direction of the groom behind him.

Then Neoma knew that he was listening, and, still talking, she went forward and put out her hand to pat his nose, then his neck.

"How beautiful you are!" she said. "I cannot believe that *Diamond*, or any other horse, is finer than you!"

Slowly, still patting his neck, she took hold of the bridle, talking and caressing him all the time as the groom, knowing now what was happening, moved forward and gently applied the poultice.

Amazingly, although the horse stiffened and Neoma thought for a moment that he might buck or rear, he stood still.

It was as if her slowly moving fingers and her soft voice mesmerised him, but finally when the poultice had been applied and she took her hand from the bridle, he still made no attempt to move.

"Now you will soon be all right," she said. "You have been good—very good!"

As she spoke, she raised her eyes from the horse to look and see if the groom had completed his task, then found, with a little start, that someone else was standing just inside the stable-door.

It was the Marquis!

"Well done, Hewson!" he said. "I see you have the poultice in place."

"Oi couldn't a-done it without the 'elp of this lady, M'Lord."

"As I saw," the Marquis remarked. "Thank you, Miss King."

Because she was shy, Neoma turned once again to pat the horse's neck.

"What is his name?" she asked.

"*Victorious*," the Marquis replied, "but up to now he has been too obstreperous to be anything but a nuisance!"

"I think really he just wants to be made a fuss of," Neoma said with a smile.

"Thank ye very much, Ma'am," Hewson said. "Oi'll know who to turn to if Oi has trouble wi' *Victorious* 'nother toim."

Neoma nearly replied that there would not be another time because she would not be here, but she merely smiled and the Marquis opened the door for her to walk into the yard.

"You obviously have an amazing way with

horses," he said. "I cannot believe that what I have just seen was an isolated incident."

"I think they know I love them," Neoma said quietly.

"I imagine you have ridden a great deal."

"Ever since I was a child, My Lord."

"I thought Standish must have found you in the country."

Neoma did not think that the Marquis meant this as a compliment.

He had obviously noticed her simple home-made gown and the fact that she did not look as sparkling and gaudy as his other guests.

She did not answer, and after a moment the Marquis went on:

"That, of course, is why I have not seen you anywhere before. How long have you been in London?"

"Only a few months," Neoma replied, thinking that this was a question she could answer truthfully.

"That accounts for it," he said, "and perhaps also for the fact that you are a very early riser."

"Perhaps I ought to have asked . . . permission to visit the stables," Neoma said, "but I wanted to be out in the fresh air, and then I was sure you would own . . . horses like . . . these."

She spoke apologetically and the Marquis replied:

"I am delighted that you should appreciate them, and may I say, considering how helpful you have been, that they are available to you at any time."

Neoma's eyes brightened for a moment, then she knew that it was only a polite way of speaking and meant nothing.

Without really thinking, she moved across the yard to the stables on the other side, which she had not yet seen.

"May I look at these horses?" she asked.

"Of course," the Marquis replied. "But I was in fact going riding. Why do you not accompany me?"

For a moment Neoma was surprised at the invitation, then everything was swept from her mind except the thought of riding one of these magnificent animals.

Since her father and mother's death she had been able to keep only two horses at the Manor and they were really too old to be worth selling.

There was a light in her eyes that was unmistakable as she said to the Marquis:

"Could I . . . really do . . . that?"

Then before he could reply she added a little hesitatingly:

"I have no . . . habit with me . . . may I ride as I . . . am?"

"It will not worry you?" he asked. "Or spoil your gown?"

She thought he would not understand if she told him that because there was no carriage at the Manor, she had ridden everywhere she had wanted to go, and always just as she was.

She would jump on the back of one of the old horses and ride to the village or across the fields to call at the farm, and it was certainly quicker and more convenient than walking.

She thought now that to ride one of the Marquis's horses would be worth spoiling all the gowns she had ever possessed.

"Please . . . let me come . . . now," she pleaded, thinking that time was passing and she must savour every moment of this marvellous opportunity.

The Marquis gave the order to Hewson and several grooms hurried to put a side-saddle on one of the finest thoroughbreds Neoma had ever seen.

In what seemed to be a flash of time she was in the saddle, and with the Marquis riding a black stallion beside her, they moved out through the other side of the stable-yard and into the Park.

Without saying anything, they started to trot, then simultaneously the horses broke into a gallop.

Neoma forgot everything but the exhilaration of being on a superb mount and knowing that she was riding faster over the turf than she had ever ridden before.

Then when they had ridden for over a mile, she realised that the Marquis was slowing his pace and she drew in her own horse.

"Thank you, thank you!" she cried, and the words came spontaneously to her lips. "That is the most wonderful thing that ever happened to me!"

"You ride superbly, but I have no need to tell you that," he said. "Who has taught you? I can hardly believe it was Standish!"

"Peregrine is a very good rider," Neoma replied, forgetting for a moment that she was not supposed to know him well.

"That does not surprise me," the Marquis said, "but you are exceptional!"

Neoma smiled but did not reply, and the Marquis asked:

"Who are you? I am interested."

"It would be very boring for me to have to talk about myself," Neoma replied, "when there are so many questions I want to ask Your Lordship."

"Questions?"

"About your house and its contents. You will think me very ignorant, but I had never heard of Syth until two days ago."

"I imagine that was when Standish asked you to accompany him."

Neoma nodded.

"I am delighted for you to be my guest," the Marquis said, "but I had the feeling last night that you were not enjoying yourself."

His words brought back all the horror and disgust that Neoma had felt.

With an effort she prevented herself from telling him the truth. Then she remembered that for Peregrine's sake she must be polite and not offend him, at least until they had found the IOU.

Because she could find nothing to say, she dug her heels sharply into her horse's sides, and as he sprang forward the Marquis could do nothing but follow her.

They rode on for some time, Neoma deliberately not slacking her speed, but finally the horses slowed to a walk and the Marquis said with a twist of his lips:

"I have a feeling, Miss King, that you have no wish to answer my question."

"No . . . My Lord."

"May I enquire why not?"

"May we talk of something . . . else?"

"What subject would you prefer?"

"I have already told you that there is a great deal I want to hear about your house."

"I have a Curator who can tell you anything you wish to know."

"I know that. Your Housekeeper told me his name is Greystone."

"So you are really interested!"

"But of course! Why should you doubt it?"

"Because most women are interested only in themselves, their clothes, their jewels, and of course their —lovers."

Neoma felt that he said the word deliberately to shock her, and the colour flooded into her face.

She did not look at the Marquis. She knew he was watching her and she felt there might be the same expression on his face as there had been last night when he had watched his guests at the dinner-table.

Before she could prevent herself, she said the first thing that came into her mind.

"Why do you spoil it?"

"What do you mean?" he asked.

"By talking like that . . . by giving parties like the . . . one you gave . . . last night."

She paused, but she felt that he was too astonished to reply and she went on recklessly:

"I have never seen such a magnificent house containing so many fabulous things, and when I looked out the window this morning I thought the sun on the lake and the deer in the Park might have been a . . . piece of Heaven."

Her voice had a little throb in it as she spoke. Then the Marquis said:

"A Heaven in which only one thing is wrong—the man who owns it!"

"I . . . did not say . . . that."

"But you thought it."

"Why are you . . . like you . . . are?"

Neoma turned her face towards the Marquis, and because his horse was moving beside hers they were in fact very near to each other, and she found that her eyes were held by his in a manner which she could not explain.

For a moment he just looked at her, and Neoma thought that her heart was beating rather more quickly than it had before.

Then the Marquis said:

"You are very frank, Miss King, and I think we ought to go back."

As he spoke he turned his horse, and Neoma did the same.

They broke into a trot and rode without speaking.

Looking at the house ahead of them, Neoma thought that she did not regret what she had said.

It was impossible to imagine that any building in the whole country could be finer or more architecturally perfect.

Its situation with the green woods behind it made it appear like a precious jewel set against velvet, and the Marquis's personal standard moving slowly in the breeze was silhouetted against the sky.

'It is the most beautiful place I have ever seen!' she thought.

Then the scene at the dinner-party the preceding night came back to make her shudder.

Still without speaking they rode up to the front door, where there were grooms waiting to take their horses.

The Marquis dismounted first, then came to Neoma to lift her from the saddle to the ground.

As he did so, she thought that he must be angry, and, thinking of Peregrine, she said in a low voice:

"I am . . . sorry if I was . . . rude. I hope you will . . . forgive me."

"I am just surprised, Miss King," the Marquis replied, and they walked up the steps side-by-side and into the Hall.

Neoma hurried to her bedroom to find not only the maid waiting there but also the Housekeeper.

"We were wondering where you were, Miss," she said, "then I saw you through the window, coming back with His Lordship."

"I got up very early and went to the stables," Neoma explained, "and His Lordship asked if I would ride with him."

"Just as you were, without a habit!" the Housekeeper said. "Well, you'd better change, Miss, and I'll have your gown pressed."

"That would be very kind of you," Neoma replied. "I am sorry to be such a trouble."

"It's no trouble, but it was quite a shock to come in so early and find you gone, so to speak. No-one gets up very early in this house, except His Lordship."

"Perhaps I should have asked what time breakfast was served," Neoma said as the maid undid her gown.

"Most of the guests, if they eat anything at all," the Housekeeper answered, "have it in their bedrooms, but we've had instructions to call everyone today because of the races. His Lordship will not wish to be kept waiting."

"No, of course not," Neoma agreed.

"What I suggest, Miss, is that you go to the Breakfast-Room when you have changed. I doubt if there'll be many to eat with you, but you will doubtless have a good appetite after your exercise."

"Now that you mention it, I am rather hungry," Neoma said with a smile, "and perhaps if I hurry there will be time for me to find Mr. Greystone and see some of the rooms before we leave."

"That's a good idea, Miss," the Housekeeper replied approvingly, "and you can trust Elise to have everything laid out for you. What were you thinking of wearing?"

"It will have to be the same gown that I wore

yesterday; I have not many gowns, and that one is the best."

"And very nice you look in it, if I may say so," the Housekeeper said. "It's a pity . . ."

She stopped suddenly, and Neoma thought that she had been about to say something derogatory about the appearance of the other ladies in the party but felt that it would be an impertinence.

Being tactful, she changed the subject and said:

"I am sure everybody will be wishing His Lordship good luck. I hope *Diamond* wins."

"We hope so too," the Housekeeper replied.

"It will be very exciting to go to the Derby," Neoma said, "and thank you very much for helping me change."

She smiled at both the maid and the Housekeeper, then went down the stairs.

She wanted to find out if Peregrine was awake, but she thought that the Housekeeper would think it very improper for her to go to a man's bedroom and therefore she did not dare to suggest it.

To her delight, however, she found Peregrine in the Breakfast-Room.

He was looking heavy-eyed and was sitting with his elbow on the table and his head on his hand.

"Peregrine!" she exclaimed. "Are you all right?"

"I feel awful!" he answered. "Why the devil did I drink so much?"

"You know it is always a mistake," Neoma said. "Try to eat something. It will make you feel better."

"It will make me feel sick!" Peregrine said sullenly.

Neoma, however, looked round and found that on a sideboard was a long array of silver dishes with a lighted wick under each to keep them warm.

There were no servants in the room and she guessed that the guests were expected to help themselves at whatever time they arrived downstairs.

She therefore fetched Peregrine the most simple dish she could find and set it in front of him, buttered a piece of toast for him, and filled his cup with coffee.

"Try to eat, dearest," she said. "It is going to be an exciting day and you will be sorry if you cannot enjoy it."

"What I want is a glass of brandy."

"Brandy?"

"It is the only thing that pulls me round after I have been 'foxed.' Charles will tell you it is the only sensible thing to drink."

As if the name conjured up his friend, Charles came into the Breakfast-Room.

He looked very much the same as Peregrine, only, if possible, his face had even less colour in it.

"God, what a night!" he exclaimed. "Neoma was the only sensible one."

"Peregrine wants some brandy," Neoma said.

"And so do I," Charles replied.

Because he obviously knew what to do, he rang a gold bell that was standing on a table and immediately a servant came into the room.

"Brandy for Mr. Standish and myself," Charles ordered.

The servant brought a decanter from a cupboard in the sideboard and poured them both what seemed to Neoma to be a quite horrifying amount of brandy.

However, after he had had a drink, Peregrine actually managed to eat something, and there certainly seemed to be more colour in his face.

As soon as the servant had left the room Neoma said:

"I want to talk to both of you."

Charles looked at her expectantly and she asked:

"How soon can we leave? I do not wish to stay one moment longer than is necessary."

"You know the answer to that," Peregrine replied. "We stay until we find what we are looking for."

He lowered his voice as he spoke, but even so, both Charles and Neoma looked apprehensively towards the door in case someone should come in and hear what they were saying.

"I do not care if we never find it!" Neoma cried. "I thought last night that none of us should be here."

Charles looked at her with understanding.

"I admit it was awful," he said, "and I was glad when I saw you slip away."

"What happened?" Peregrine asked. "I cannot remember much about it."

"I expect most people say the same," Charles answered, "and a good thing, too, if you ask me."

"Why does he have those ... terrible women here?" Neoma asked in a low voice. "And why does he let his friends get so drunk and disgusting?"

"I suppose that is what he likes," Charles replied.

There seemed to be no other answer, Neoma told herself, but she could not believe that a man who could encourage such depravity was the same man who had just ridden beside her in a manner which she knew would have gained her father's approval.

"You did not answer my question," she said aloud. "When can we leave?"

"I suppose on Friday," Charles answered. "Most of the men, at any rate, will want to go racing again tomorrow."

Neoma thought with a sinking of her heart that that meant there were two more nights to get through.

"Perhaps we could leave in the evening after the races have finished?" she suggested.

"What would be the point of that?" Peregrine asked. "Besides, I have ordered the carriage to be here on Friday morning."

Neoma was about to expostulate that it was too long to stay, when several other guests came into the Breakfast-Room, and because she had finished she rose and went in search of Mr. Greystone.

She found him in a palatial office hung with maps and surrounded by files and strong-boxes, all bearing the Marquis's crest.

Rather shyly she introduced herself, and Mr. Greystone was immediately most encouraging.

"I can understand your interest, Miss King," he said, "but it would take many hours to view the whole house, which, if I may say so, is one of the finest in the country."

He spoke proudly and continued:

"But as you say you have only a short time now before you leave for the races, I suggest we look at the nearest rooms to this, and then when you have a little more time at your disposal, perhaps we can cover the State-Rooms and of course the Chapel."

"There is a Chapel?" Neoma asked with interest.

"Yes indeed," Mr. Greystone replied. "It was built before Vanburgh pulled down the original Mansion to build the one you see now."

"Is the Chapel near this room?"

"Quite near."

"Then could we go and see that first?"

Neoma felt that the presence of a Chapel somewhat mitigated the evil that had frightened her last night.

"Is it in use?" she asked as she and Mr. Greystone walked along the corridor outside his office.

"Yes indeed," he replied. "The Marquis's private Chaplain holds a Service every Sunday."

Neoma looked at him in astonishment before she said:

"The Marquis has a private Chaplain?"

"Yes. It is quite usual where there is a Chapel attached to a house of this size, and of course it is far more convenient for the servants to attend a Service here than to walk a mile to the village Church."

"Yes, I can understand that," Neoma agreed.

They reached the Chapel and she looked at it with delight.

It was very old, as Mr. Greystone had said, and the stained-glass window over the altar had been there since 1680.

The magnificent pews had been carved at the same time, and the one occupied by the Marquis was as regal as if he were a King.

The altar was of alabaster, and all round the walls were paintings by Laguerre and Ricard of the Life of Christ.

But Neoma could only think that this was a place of sanctity, a small House of God enclosed in a building which must have forgotten Him.

Because she wished to pray, she knelt down in one of the pews on a red velvet hassock and therefore did not see the look of surprise on Mr. Greystone's face.

She prayed for some minutes, asking God's help and begging her mother to assist Peregrine and most of all to prevent him from gambling when he had no money.

"Help us, God; help us, Mama," she prayed as she had prayed before, then added one of the simple prayers that she had said as a child.

She rose to her feet and Mr. Greystone thought that there was a very sweet expression on her face and it was a shame that such a lovely, spiritual-looking girl should have embarked so early in life on a career which could only lead eventually to despair.

He said nothing, but escorted Neoma back the way they had come, to show her one very attractive Sitting-Room before it was time for her to dress for the races.

When she came down the stairs again, the chatter of voices sounded very out of keeping with the beauty of the Hall, and the gowns of the ladies clashed unpleasantly with the paintings which had been done, Mr. Greystone had told her, also by Laguerre.

Neoma saw Peregrine amongst the crowd and went quickly to his side, only to see with a feeling of consternation that he already had a glass of champagne in his hand, as had everybody else.

"Do not drink any more," she begged in a low voice.

He smiled at her and said:

"I am all right. I am feeling better already."

It was obvious that the champagne had also revived everyone else, and they all went out through the front door to where a large coach was waiting.

To Neoma's surprise, although she might have expected it, the Marquis intended to tool the magnificent team of horses that drew it.

His guests all climbed up onto the top of the coach, where special seats had been constructed on the roof, while the servants sat inside.

There were shouts and cries of: "Tally Ho!" as the coach set off, and Neoma, seated beside Peregrine, enjoyed from such a height an excellent view of the garden and the lake.

Then as they drove up the drive she realised that someone was changing places with the man who had been seated on her other side, and with a sinking of her heart she saw that it was Lord Dadchett.

He was inevitably close to her and she moved as near as she could to Peregrine.

"You are looking entrancing this morning, Miss King," Lord Dadchett said. "Are you hoping to make your fortune on the races?"

"I cannot afford to gamble, My Lord," Neoma said in a stiff little voice.

"No, of course not," he replied, "so you must allow me to back what horses you fancy, and perhaps together we shall make a large fortune."

"It is very kind of Your Lordship, but the answer is no," Neoma said. "I do not approve of gambling."

"That is certainly an original statement from someone like yourself," Lord Dadchett replied.

Neoma turned her head to talk to Peregrine, but unfortunately he was discussing the merits of the various horses with a gentleman who was sitting in front of him, and Lord Dadchett said:

"If you are not interested in racing, perhaps you would like me to tell you the story of Epsom and how the famous Epsom Salts were discovered."

It was annoying, Neoma thought, that that was something she would be interested to hear and that Lord Dadchett should be aware of it.

Because she thought it was a safer subject then herself and her likes and dislikes, she listened as he explained that in 1618 a man called Henry Whicker took his cattle to drink from a spring that he had found in a field at Epsom.

"The beasts refused to drink," Lord Dadchett said,

"and when Whicker tasted the water, he found it distinctly unpleasant."

His face seemed to Neoma to come menacingly nearer as he went on:

"However, in twenty years the gluttons at the Stuart Court in London were journeying to Epsom to take the waters to purge their livers. I think you will agree, Miss King, that it is something quite a number of our fellow-guests should do this morning."

Neoma had no wish to discuss such things with Lord Dadchett or anyone else, and he went on:

"Obviously the Courtiers wanted entertainment while they took the cure, and a whole collection of Gaming-Houses and Cock-pits grew up, and what should be more natural than that they should build a race-course?"

Because she really found it interesting, Neoma exclaimed:

"So that was how the racing started!"

"I thought it would amuse you," Lord Dadchett said, "and I can think of many other things which would amuse you even more—if you were kind to me."

There was a note in his voice that Neoma did not like, and she said quickly:

"But how did the race come to be called the Derby?"

"Epsom might have remained just a small meeting," Lord Dadchett replied, "if the twenty-one-year-old future Earl of Derby had not taken the lease of a converted ale-house called The Oaks."

He saw that Neoma recognised the name, and he continued:

"Yes, that was the origin of the Oaks Stakes, when the Earl allowed the name of his house to be given to one of the Epsom races."

"That is interesting!" Neoma was forced to admit.

"The promoters of the Oaks decided on a race of one-and-a-half miles for three-year-old fillies," Lord Dadchett continued, "and the following year, in 1780, the Earl and his friends decided that there should be a similar race for all three-year-olds, and that was how the Derby Stakes were instituted."

He smiled unpleasantly, Neoma thought, as he added:

"Now that I have pleased you, tell me how you are going to reciprocate by pleasing me."

"I do not know . . . what you . . . mean."

"I think you do," he said, "and tonight, instead of slipping away after dinner, you must let me show you some of the beauties of Syth. The Picture-Gallery is well worth a visit."

The way he spoke made Neoma decide that tonight she would go to bed even earlier than she had done the night before.

Fortunately, at this moment they joined a stream of traffic moving towards the Downs and there was so much to look at and to exclaim about that it was impossible for Lord Dadchett to go on whispering in her ear.

The road was crowded with every sort of vehicle that could be pulled by a horse or a donkey.

There were smart four-in-hand coaches whose posthorns and drivers cursed the costermongers in their carts, and overloaded broughams, waggonettes, and barouches.

There was a long queue at a turnpike-house as the drivers paid their dues, but fortunately as Syth was near to the Downs they had not far to go in such congestion.

Now to Neoma's delight she found that the entertainers who did not wish to stand the competition on the hill had set up their coconut-shies and other attractions by the side of the road.

Tumblers and acrobats were begging pennies from the slowly moving cavalcade and the guests on the Marquis's coach threw them money just for the fun of seeing them scramble in the dust for it.

At last they were on the open ground and as the carriages swung up the slopes of the hill in style, with horns blowing, they were greeted with applause by those on foot.

Neoma saw a huge Stand which Peregrine told

her had only been completed that very year, at a cost of twenty thousand pounds.

It appeared to be already filled with people, and opposite it and on each side the coaches and carriages were taking up their positions to watch the races.

It seemed to Neoma that there was such a hurly-burly that she wondered if when the time came the horses would ever get through.

But for the moment she was entranced by the cries of the touts and tipsters and the spillers outside the booths whose owners wore silk waist-coats and hats with huge ostrich-plumes.

Outside the gambling-pits there were servants in gorgeous liveries, wheedling and encouraging the suckers in with a promise of riches.

And there was music everywhere. Some of the performers were gypsy-fiddlers and as they played, their women moved round, telling fortunes and asking for their palms to be crossed with silver.

Standing up on the coach, which the Marquis had put into an excellent position near the new Stand, Neoma could see boxing-booths with crews of fighters, many of them, Peregrine said, famous old champions with flattened noses and battered faces who were earning money the only way they knew.

Conjurers performed endless tricks, and ventriloquists argued with their dummies, all encircled by a crowd of vacant-looking country-folk and hundreds of ragged children.

"Watch out for pick-pockets," Charles said when Peregrine said he wished to leave the coach.

"They will get nothing from me!" Peregrine replied, and asked Neoma, "Are you coming?"

"Yes, of course," she answered, well aware that Lord Dadchett would be at her side if she was left alone.

There was, however, such a crowd that Peregrine soon decided to return to the coach, and he and Neoma found that luncheon had been laid out in their absence.

The servants had provided tables and chairs and there were drinks of every sort and description, including, of course, champagne, arranged on a separate table out of the sun.

It was, Neoma thought, a fantastic feast, with every delicious dish of which she had ever heard.

There was cold salmon, turkey, brawn, ox-tongue, a pig's head, and of course a profusion of sweet puddings that looked as if they might melt in the sun.

Although she was hungry, she wondered if many of the other guests would feel like having a large meal. But, perhaps stimulated by the wine, they managed to eat a great deal, and the gentlemen threw chicken-legs and pieces of tongue and ham to the children who watched with hungry eyes.

They were so long over luncheon that they saw the first two races with glasses still in their hands.

Then came the Derby Stakes and Peregrine said that they must go to the Paddock and look at the horses.

Neoma was only too willing, and they watched them being led round and round by their grooms while the jockeys stood in the centre of the ring, talking to their owners.

There were also a number of very smartly dressed women accompanied by resplendent gentlemen.

None of them, Neoma thought, was as outstanding as the Marquis. She had seen him stroll off half-way through the luncheon, accompanied by Vicky Vale.

She was looking fantastic and wearing what Neoma secretly thought was a very vulgar display of jewellery for a race-meeting.

The yellow feathers in her bonnet and the yellow silk shawl she wore draped round her shoulders made her outstanding even in such a large crowd, and Neoma imagined that the Marquis wished to parade her in front of his friends.

At the moment, however, she was concerned only with the horses.

"That is *Diamond*," Peregrine said as a horse passed, looking in the peak of condition, and then Charles joined them.

"Let us put every penny we have on *Diamond*,"

he said to Peregrine. "We will get rotten odds, but we might as well try and make a bit."

"No," Neoma said in a frightened voice. "You must not do that."

"Why not?" Peregrine asked.

She looked at *Diamond*, who was not a little distance away from them. Then she said:

"He will not win!"

"What on earth do you mean?" Charles enquired. "*Diamond* is bound to win! No other horse has a chance against him!"

Neoma did not reply for a moment. Then she said in a low voice:

"I am sure, absolutely sure, that that one will be the winner."

As she spoke she pointed, and both men looked at her in astonishment.

"It is impossible!" Charles exclaimed.

He drew out his race-card as he spoke.

"Let me see, *Sailor* is owned by T. Thornhill Esquire, and the jockey is S. Chifney. If you ask me, he hasn't a chance against *Diamond*."

"Nevertheless, *Diamond* will not win," Neoma insisted.

"I find that a very extraordinary statement from one of my guests," a voice said.

Neoma gave a little start and knew, without turning her head, who had spoken.

"That is exactly what I said, My Lord," Peregrine said. "There is no other horse in the race worth mentioning."

"That is what I would like to think," the Marquis replied. "At the same time, I wish to know why Miss King has no confidence in *Diamond*."

Neoma raised her eyes to his and found it difficult to reply.

Then she said:

"I am sorry ... and of course I may be wrong ... but I just feel that *Sailor* will be the winner."

"That is ridiculous and you know it!" Peregrine said sharply.

As he spoke, he realised that his tone was hardly what he would have used to the "lady-friend" which Neoma was supposed to be.

"But of course we are all entitled to our own opinions," he finished lamely.

The Marquis's eyes were still on Neoma.

"Why do you feel like that, Miss King?"

"It is . . . something I cannot . . . explain," she said, speaking only to him. "It is the same feeling that I had this morning when I knew I could control *Victorious* . . . nevertheless, I may be . . . wrong."

"I doubt it," the Marquis said unexpectedly, "and I advise you gentlemen to listen to Miss King. She is too experienced with horses to make a mistake."

As he spoke, he walked away, leaving both Peregrine and Charles gaping after him.

"Did you hear what he said?" Peregrine asked at length.

"I heard!" Charles replied. "Perhaps we had better do as he says."

"But *Sailor*! Who has ever heard of that horse?" Peregrine exclaimed.

"Please . . . please do not bet," Neoma begged. "We cannot . . . afford it, and if you lose all your money, Charles, we shall have to leave without tipping the servants, and you know how ignominious that will be."

Charles shrugged his shoulders, then said:

"You have told me to back *Sailor* and so has the Marquis. Who am I to argue?"

"Why should Neoma know anything about it?" Peregrine interposed. "Obviously the Marquis was only being polite."

"Polite?" Charles repeated. "The Marquis? Have you ever known him to speak like that before?"

"I had never heard him speak at all until the other night."

"Well, you know his reputation at White's!"

"Yes, but still . . ."

Charles made up his mind.

"It is my money and I am going to do as I have been told."

"Not . . . all of it . . . please. . . not all of it!" Neoma begged.

"Very well," Charles conceded, "half; and if we lose, the other half gets us home."

"That has some sense in it," Neoma agreed.

Charles moved away and was lost in the crowd and Peregrine turned angrily to his sister.

"If you ask me, you are making a fool of yourself. We at least had a chance to increase our money on *Diamond*, and the Marquis is going to be laughing when he leads him in!"

Neoma did not reply.

She could understand what Peregrine was feeling, but some deep conviction in herself remained unchanged.

There was a sudden cry of: "They're off!" and Peregrine hurried Neoma to the edge of the course and they found a place to stand near the winning post

She braced herself tensely to watch the race, but they learnt a few minutes later that it had been a false start and the horses had been called back.

"Do not get excited!" Peregrine warned. "I am told there are sometimes up to twenty false starts before they really get going."

"I do not think I could bear it!" Neoma replied.

She spoke with such intensity in her voice that Peregrine suddenly smiled and slipped his arm through hers.

"Cheer up!" he said. "Once they are really off, the whole thing will be over in less than three minutes. Somebody said last night that the Derby means 'immortality for a horse in two minutes and forty-five seconds.' "

It seemed, however, a century before finally a triumphant cry went up from the crowd and Neoma knew that the flag was down and they were away.

She could hear the thunder of their hoofs almost before she saw them coming round Tattenham Corner, and then she held her breath.

Now she would know if she had been right or wrong, and she found herself praying that for all their sakes she had been right.

Chapter Four

"How did you know? How did you guess?"

Peregrine kept asking the same questions, and Charles, when he came back smiling with delight, did the same.

All Neoma could reply was that she had no real explanation of the feeling she had had about *Diamond* and *Sailor*.

"Well, at least we shall go home with some money jingling in our pockets," Charles said with delight.

"I hope to go home with a good deal more than that," Peregrine replied.

Both Charles and Neoma felt guilty because for the moment they had forgotten the two-thousand-pound IOU which hung over their heads like the sword of Damocles.

As they turned to walk away from the winning-post towards the coach, Neoma said pleadingly:

"Please do not tell anyone ... what happened."

"No. We would be wise to keep our mouths shut," Peregrine agreed. "No-one will be at all pleased to learn that we have won when they will undoubtedly have backed *Diamond* to the hilt."

"The Marquis knows," Charles remarked.

"We can hardly ask him to keep silent," Peregrine answered, "but perhaps he will have the good sense not to say anything."

Neoma found herself saying a little prayer that they would not be greeted with reproaches and recriminations because they had not told the others that Sailor was likely to be the winner.

There was in fact an atmosphere of gloom about the whole party as they boarded the coach, ready to leave the race-course.

The Marquis had said on the way to the Downs that he intended to leave after the Derby for the simple reason that if they waited any longer the road would be congested to the point where it might take them hours to get back to Syth.

Even so, it was difficult for anyone to drive, even a man as experienced as the Marquis, through the crowded traffic and race-goers trudging in slow procession away from the Downs.

Every Inn they passed was filled to overflowing with people needing to fortify themselves before they attempted the long journey back to London.

This meant that they moved about unsteadily in the road outside the Inn, getting in the way of the horses and anyone else who was trying to leave behind the huge crowds on the hill.

There seemed to be more ragged children than ever, some of them looking so thin and emaciated that Neoma longed to be able to give them all a feast such as had been laid out at luncheon-time.

She also listened to the gentlemen in the party exclaiming over the comfort and facilities of the new Stand.

One of them said:

"I was taken over the whole place and I must say I think they have done an excellent job, especially in the Refreshment-Salon."

"You mean that one can actually eat on the Stand?" someone asked.

"There is plenty to tempt the appetite," the first speaker replied. "Rows of spits were turning dozens of joints before a blazing fire. I was told that the caterers had brought in one hundred thirty legs-of-lamb, sixty-five saddles, one hundred sirloins-of-beef, besides four hundred lobsters and innumerable other things."

Neoma longed to ask what would be done with

the food that was left over and if there was a chance
of the beggar-children having any, but she was too
shy to ask.

Also, she was very anxious not to draw attention to herself in case the Marquis should then say that
in the whole party she was the only person who had
not been convinced that *Diamond* would bring home
the Derby Stakes.

As she listened to Vicky Vale and all the other
women commiserating with him, she held her breath
just in case he should tell them what he had overheard her saying.

To her relief, he appeared to be concentrating
on his driving and paying little attention to anyone.

Amongst the gentlemen on the coach there were
unconcealed mutters and grumbles of dissatisfaction
and disappointment.

"It is the worst Derby Day I have ever known!"
she heard Lord Dadchett murmur. "It has cost me a
packet!"

"It has cost me a damned sight more than that,"
declared the Member of Parliament who had been
sitting next to Neoma at dinner the preceding night.

There was one blessing, she thought, and that
was that because Lord Dadchett was so discomfited
by the performance of his host's horse, he was making
no effort to engage her attention as he had done in
the morning.

Instead, the men were now mostly sitting together
discussing their racing losses, while the women filled
the seat behind Neoma without a man amongst them.

"I imagine this says good-bye to the necklace I
was hoping Henry'd give me," Neoma heard one
woman say.

"I'll be lucky if I get my rent paid!" another replied. "This is the climax of a long run of losses as
far as His Lordship's concerned!"

"I told you, Lotty, to look round for someone
else," a woman remarked.

Lotty yawned.

"I suppose that's what it'll come to. But I've grown used to the old boy, and he's generous enough when he's got anything to be generous with."

Neoma, listening to the women, did not understand why they expected the men who had brought them to Syth to give them so much.

Then she remembered how Avril had told her that she would look after Charles's money, and she found herself finding it even more incomprehensible.

She had not forgotten that Peregrine had said that even if he had known a woman whom he could bring, on the Marquis's invitation, he would not be able to pay her.

It seemed to Neoma amazing that women who knew that they would be entertained in what seemed to her to be such magnificent circumstances should actually expect necklaces and cash as well.

Then she told herself that it must be because the majority of them were actresses and therefore being away from London perhaps they would lose the salary they would have been paid at the Theatres.

This seemed the obvious explanation, but she thought that they must have very important roles to earn the equivalent of a diamond necklace or the rent of a house.

She was, however, very ignorant on such matters. Actresses might command hundreds of pounds a week for all she knew.

She remembered reading in the newspapers that celebrities like Mrs. Siddons had been given "Benefits," which her father had told her meant that all the proceeds of that particular performance were handed over entirely to the actor or actress for whom it was arranged.

It was therefore apparent, she thought, that the women talking behind her were actresses of some note, and she determined to try to learn their names so that even if Peregrine could not take her to the Theatre, she would be able to follow their careers in the theatrical-columns of the newspapers.

She thought that perhaps when they got home she

would be able to talk to Peregrine about the party
and get him to explain to her many of the things she
found puzzling.

The most puzzling of all was the Marquis himself.

She thought he must still be angry with her for
being so outspoken when she had asked him why he
behaved as he did.

In retrospect she felt that it had not only been
an indiscreet and impertinent question but one which
might react unfavourably on Peregrine.

'Perhaps I should be very polite and humble to
make up,' she thought.

Then she knew it was unlikely that she would
ever again be able to talk intimately with the Marquis
as she had done that morning.

She wondered if there was any chance of her
ever riding with him again, then decided that he would
certainly not want her after what he called her "frank-
ness."

'How could I have been so stupid?' she wondered.

But she told herself that it was not of the least
consequence. The day after tomorrow they would be
leaving and that would be the last time she would
ever see the Marquis.

'Unless of course . . .'

She stopped the train of her thoughts because
they frightened her.

Supposing they could not find the IOU? Supposing Peregrine had to humiliate himself by offering the
Marquis the Manor because it was quite impossible
for him to find the sum he owed?

In which case, Neoma thought, she might have
to go down on her knees to ask him if she might keep
just a few of her mother's personal possessions which
she could not bear to lose.

"Why, oh why," she asked herself, "are we in
this terrible position?"

Then knew the answer was that her father had
been very foolish over money, and at the same time
Peregrine had been brought up to have expensive
tastes.

She sighed involuntarily, and Charles, sitting beside her, said:

"You sound gloomy."

Before Neoma could reply, Avril, who was on the other side of him, said crossly:

"She's got a lot to be gloomy about—as I have! Why couldn't the Marquis's stupid horse win as everybody said it would?"

Avril's voice rose, and Charles, giving an uncomfortable glance at the Marquis's back, said:

"Be careful! I do not expect that our host is too pleased at being a loser."

"What happened to the horse anyway?" Avril enquired.

"It was just not fast enough and *Sailor* beat him to the post," Charles replied.

"Well, as far as I'm concerned it's a pity that I don't know the owner of *Sailor!*" Avril snapped.

Neoma thought that she was deliberately being unpleasant to Charles.

They reached Syth and as they drove down the drive she could think of nothing but the beauty of the house ahead of her.

Once again she found herself wondering how the Marquis could be the owner of anything so exquisite and fill it with people who not only were unworthy of such a background but, what was more, did not even appreciate it.

Ever since they had arrived at Syth, Neoma had not seen one of the Marquis's guests admiring the pictures, the statues, or the superb furniture.

As she thought of it, she realised with a feeling of delight that as they were home so early, there would be plenty of time before dinner to see more of the house.

She was so excited by the idea that she hurried to her bedroom to leave her bonnet and her gloves, and then, determined that no-one should stop her, she sped down the corridor which led to Mr. Greystone's office.

He was bent over his desk, writing, but he looked up with a smile as she entered.

"We are back, Mr. Greystone!" Neoma said breathlessly. "Have you the time to show me more of the house?"

There was an anxious look in her eyes which Mr. Greystone did not miss, and he replied:

"His Lordship's affairs will have to wait, Miss King, and we will take up our tour of the house where we left off."

"Oh, thank you! Thank you!" Neoma cried.

There was no doubt that Mr. Greystone not only loved the house—Neoma learnt that he had worked there for nearly twenty years—but he knew every detail about it.

He showed her the magnificent room painted by James Thornhill in 1705, after which he took her to the State-Music-Room and the State-Bedroom which had been used the preceding year when the Regent had visited Syth.

"Was the Marquis pleased to have him as a guest?" Neoma enquired.

There was just a moment's hesitation before Mr. Greystone replied:

"His Lordship did not invite His Royal Highness. He insisted on coming to Syth, and this is the third time he has done so."

"I hear that the Marquis's treasures make him green with envy."

"I think that is the truth, and I have a feeling that in some instances he is trying to vie with us in his own residences."

"That must prove exceedingly difficult," Neoma said with a smile.

She was looking at the enormous four-poster bed with its carved canopy, and the fantastic ceiling which depicted Dawn chasing away the Night and had land-scaped scenes painted in the covings, with groups of figures in the corners.

It was all so lovely that she added:

"It is a wonderful experience just to look at this ceiling."

"I feel that about so many things in Syth," Mr. Greystone agreed.

"I have run out of adjectives with which to describe all I see," Neoma said.

A voice that was not Mr. Greystone's replied:

"Then you must allow me to supply you with some."

She started and turned to see that Lord Dadchett had come into the State-Bedroom.

She looked at him uncomfortably and he said to Mr. Greystone:

"I regret having to interrupt what I imagine is a well-conducted tour of the house, but His Lordship requires you immediately in the Library."

Mr. Greystone seemed to hesitate for a moment, and Lord Dadchett, looking at him, repeated:

"I said—immediately!"

As if he accepted the inevitable, Mr. Greystone bowed and said to Neoma:

"Will you excuse me, Miss King? I hope I shall not be away for long."

"No, please come back," Neoma said, "or perhaps I should come with you?"

She walked towards the door, but Lord Dadchett barred her.

"There is no need for you to give up your tour," he said. "I am only too willing to be your guide, and I assure you I know Syth well and can tell you everything you wish to know."

"It is very kind of Your Lordship," Neoma replied. "At the same time, Mr. Greystone has been so obliging in teaching me so much that I would rather not lose him."

"Greystone must obey his Master," Lord Dadchett said.

As he spoke, Neoma realised that Mr. Greystone had left the State-Bedroom.

Lord Dadchett looked at her with a smile on his rather thick lips.

"I have a feeling you have been trying to avoid me," he said, "and that is something I have no intention of allowing you to do."

"It is getting late," Neoma said quickly, "and I think I should go and look for Mr. Standish."

"Your friend is quite happy without you," Lord Dadchett replied. "In fact I left him drinking away the sorrows of his losses with the rest of the party."

Neoma hoped that Peregrine would not drink too much, but it was with a sense of relief that she realised that no-one knew that he and Charles were not losers on the Derby.

"So that leaves the way clear," Lord Dadchett was saying, "for you and me to have the little chat which you promised me."

"I promised nothing of the . . . sort!" Neoma retorted.

"Well, I promised it to myself, and that amounts to very much the same thing. I want to talk to you, and I want a great many other things as well."

There was an expression in his eyes which made Neoma alarmed, and she said:

"I do not wish to talk, I wish to look at the house and particularly to see the pictures in the Hall."

She thought, as she spoke, that this was rather a clever move on her part, because in the Hall there were servants and it would be impossible for Lord Dadchett to dare to be too familiar when there were a number of footmen standing about.

As he obviously guessed her intention, he laughed.

"You have seen the Hall," he said, "and instead I am delighted to show you this room and especially its very comfortable bed."

He put out his arm towards her as he spoke, and though Neoma moved quickly to avoid him, he caught hold of her wrist.

"You have played with me long enough," he said. "Let us call a truce, for I have something important to say to you."

"Let me go!" Neoma cried. "I do not like being kept here against my will."

"I want to keep you here," Lord Dadchett answered. "I also want you to listen to me, and I think you would be wise to do so."

"Wise?" Neoma enquired.

"Standish is too young and obviously not rich

A Personal Invitation from Barbara Cartland

Dear Reader,

I have formed the Barbara Cartland "Health and Happiness Club" so that I can share with you my sensational discoveries on beauty, health, love and romance, which is both physical and spiritual.

I will communicate with you through a series of newsletters throughout the year which will serve as a forum for you to tell me what you personally have felt, and you will also be able to learn the thoughts and feelings of other members who join me in my "Search for Rainbows." I will be thrilled to know you wish to participate.

In addition, the Health and Happiness Club will make available to members only, the finest quality health and beauty care products personally selected by me.

Do please join my Health and Happiness Club. Together we will find the secrets which bring rapture and ecstasy to my heroines and point the way to true happiness.

Yours,

FREE Membership Offer

Health & Happiness Club

Dear Barbara,

Please enroll me as a charter member in the Barbara Cartland "Health and Happiness Club." My membership application appears on the form below (or on a plain piece of paper).

I look forward to receiving the first in a series of your newsletters and learning about your sensational discoveries on beauty, health, love and romance.

I understand that the newsletters and membership in your club are <u>free</u>.

* * *

Kindly send your membership application to:
Health and Happiness Club, Inc.
Two Penn Plaza
New York, N. Y. 10001

NAME_____

ADDRESS_____

CITY_____

STATE_____ ZIP_____

Allow 2 weeks for delivery of the first newsletter.

enough to give you all you deserve," Lord Dadchett said. "I can promise you that I am a far more attractive proposition from every point of view."

For a moment Neoma looked at him incredulously, not quite understanding what he was suggesting.

Then, before she could explain to herself what he was suggesting, he pulled her nearer to him, and before she could prevent it, both his arms were round her.

"You are very attractive," he said. "In fact you excite me as I have not been excited for a very long time."

"Let me go!" Neoma cried.

As she spoke, she realised that Lord Dadchett intended to kiss her, and she turned her head sharply away from him.

He was, however, holding her so close against him that she found it difficult to move.

She felt a sudden, rising panic because he was imprisoning her, and however hard she fought against him, her strength was in no way the equal of his.

She tried to struggle and he laughed.

"Still fighting me?" he asked. "Well, I find that a novelty, at any rate! And you will amuse me even more when you finally capitulate."

"Let me . . . go!" Neoma cried again.

She pushed him away from her with all her strength, but as she did so she found that his arms still kept her captive.

"We will talk about it when you have given me a kiss," Lord Dadchett said.

Again his lips came nearer, and Neoma flung back her head and avoided him.

Lord Dadchett merely increased the pressure of his arms, and now she knew that he was pulling her relentlessly closer and closer and there was little she could do about it.

The idea of him kissing her was so horrifying and at the same time so revolting that because she felt helpless, there was nothing she could do but scream.

She screamed and screamed again, but it was as

if her efforts to escape merely increased Lord Dadchett's determination, and then she felt his lips on her
cheek.

Even as she knew despairingly that it was only
a question of time before he would kiss her mouth,
a voice from the doorway said sharply:

"Poaching on someone else's preserves, George?"

With a leap of her heart Neoma realised that the
Marquis was there and had saved her when she had
thought she was utterly lost.

Lord Dadchett's arms relaxed and with a last desperate struggle she was free of him. Running across
the room, she flung herself against the Marquis and
held on to him from sheer relief.

The Marquis put one arm round her and he could
feel her trembling against him as she hid her face
against his shoulder.

Lord Dadchett turned round angrily.

"What the hell do you want?" he enquired.

"I can hardly allow my guests to scream and not
come to their rescue," the Marquis replied.

"I do not interfere in your affairs," Lord Dadchett said, "and I do not expect you to interfere in
mine."

"Yours or Standish's?" the Marquis enquired.

Neoma was suddenly aware that she was holding
on to the Marquis and now was free of Lord Dadchett.

With an effort she moved away from him, saying a little incoherently:

"Please ... may I ... go ... and ... thank you."

Without waiting to hear his reply, she went from
the State-Bedroom, and as soon as she was in the corridor she ran frantically in the direction of her own
bedroom.

The Marquis did not move from the position he
had assumed at the end of the room and merely said
to Lord Dadchett:

"My Curator told me you said I had sent for him,
which was untrue."

"Good God, Rosyth," Lord Dadchett replied, "if
I take a fancy to some little Cyprian who has been

brought here by somebody else, why the devil should you care?"

"The girl is very young and obviously has no wish to exchange Standish's protection for yours."

"She will soon learn on which side her bread is buttered," Lord Dadchett answered. "Standish obviously has no money and I am quite prepared to set her up in style. She attracts me."

"I presume she has some say in the matter?" the Marquis retorted. "The screams I heard as I came into the room inclined me to think she is not anxious to change partners."

"I will convince her," Lord Dadchett said, "and you keep out of this. You have Vicky. What more can you want?"

The Marquis was silent for a moment, then he said:

"Leave Miss King alone while you are in my house, and that is not a request—it is an order!"

Lord Dadchett stared at the Marquis incredulously before he asked:

"What the devil has got into you? You have never, to my knowledge, interfered before in whatever takes place at your sometimes outrageous parties."

The Marquis merely replied:

"I have told you—leave her alone!"

"And if I do not obey you?" Lord Dadchett asked defiantly.

"I think you will find me an unpleasant enemy," the Marquis answered, and turned and walked from the room.

Lord Dadchett followed, with an expression of surprise on his face.

The Marquis, he thought, was always unaccountable, but there was certainly no explanation he could think of as to why in this particular instance he should wish to protect an unknown, unfledged young woman who was very different in every way from his usual taste in such creatures.

At the same time, there had been a steely note in his voice which told Lord Dadchett that he meant what he said.

There was certainly no point, he told himself, in annoying the Marquis. All the same, he had no intention of giving up the chase.

"As soon as we leave Syth," he told himself, "I will have a talk with Standish. I have a feeling I can make him see sense."

The idea was a salve to his pride, and as he walked down the stairs he told himself that he was by no means discouraged in his pursuit of a "bit o' muslin" who attracted him in a manner he could not explain.

*   *   *

Neoma reached her bedroom and found that she was still trembling and her heart was beating violently.

She had never thought it possible that she would have to pit her strength against that of a man and know that she had no chance of escaping from him.

She remembered how she had thought Lord Dadchett was dangerous from the first moment she had met him and that Peregrine had repeatedly warned her against him.

How could she have imagined for one moment, she asked herself, that he would pursue her when she was going round the house and send Mr. Greystone away so that she was completely at his mercy?

Inside her bedroom, she sat down on a chair, feeling that she must get her breath and somehow stop herself from feeling so frightened.

'If only we could go home now,' she thought.

She wondered how she could possibly get through the evening knowing that Lord Dadchett would be at dinner and perhaps scheming how to trap her again into being alone with him.

She remembered how he had told her that he wanted to show her the Picture-Gallery, and she shuddered at the thought of what might have happened if the Marquis had not come in at exactly the right moment.

"I hate him!" she told herself. "And I hate everybody in this house! If only we could leave!"

Then she had a sudden idea, and when about fifteen minutes later Elsie came to prepare her bath and get out her things for the evening, she sent the maid in search of the Housekeeper.

When she arrived, rustling in her black silk dress, Neoma said:

"I am sorry to bother you, but I wonder if it would be possible for me to have dinner up here tonight. I have rather a headache after the noise and heat of the race-course, but I would not wish to put anyone out by not going downstairs."

"I'm sure His Lordship will understand," the Housekeeper replied. "It will be quite easy, Miss, to have a tray brought up for you. I'll give the order now, while Elsie prepares your bath."

"Thank you very much," Neoma said. "You are quite certain it will be all right?"

"Now don't you worry, Miss," the Housekeeper replied in a kinder tone than she had used to her before. "You get into bed and leave everything to me."

"Thank you," Neoma said.

She waited until the Housekeeper had bustled away, then she sat down at the *Secretaire* in the corner of the bedroom and quickly wrote a note to Peregrine.

She knew it would be a mistake to tell him about Lord Dadchett or the Marquis. Instead, she just said that she had a headache and had no wish to go downstairs to sit through another dinner like the one last night.

She begged him not to drink too much; then, having signed her name, she added:

"Destroy this letter as soon as you have read it."

She knew it was a wise precaution, because if she was not careful in what she wrote, the servants might see it and think perhaps it was not the sort of letter they would expect her to write to a young man.

She sealed the letter, and then, making sure that Elsie was shut in the dressing-room where she was preparing her bath, she quickly opened the communicating-doors between their bedrooms and threw the letter just inside.

'The valet will find it,' she thought, 'and put it on the dressing-table.'

Then with a feeling of relief that she had not to suffer another ghastly dinner like the one last night, she undressed and had her bath.

A delicious dinner was sent up to her, and when she had eaten far more than anyone with a bad headache was likely to do, Neoma knew that she was in fact quite tired.

However, she could not resist asking the House-keeper, who had come in to see if she was all right, if there were any books she could read.

"Books, Miss?"

"I think I would just like to read for a little while before I go to sleep," Neoma explained, "but I do not wish to be any trouble."

"It's no trouble, Miss," the Housekeeper replied, "but it's not often that His Lordship's lady-guests ask for anything to read."

"I spend a great deal of time reading," Neoma answered, "and I am sure that there are many wonderful books in a house like this. Mr. Greystone has promised to show me the Library, but I wanted to see the State-Rooms first."

"Well, you have a treat coming to you," the Housekeeper said. "The Library is one of the finest rooms in the house and I believe I am right in saying that there are over twenty thousand books in it."

"Twenty thousand!" Neoma exclaimed. "I would like to read all of them!"

"I think that would mean your staying here for the rest of your life, Miss."

"As that is impossible, I shall be content with just one," Neoma said with a smile.

"There are more than that on this floor," the Housekeeper replied. "You get into bed, Miss, and I'll bring you some."

She went away, and when she came back her arms were filled with books.

Neoma sat up excitedly.

"How kind you are!" she exclaimed. "This is very exciting for me!"

The Housekeeper put the books down on the table beside her and said:

"As a matter of fact, Miss, these are from His Lordship's private Sitting-Room. His valet let me have them."

"Will His Lordship mind?" Neoma asked apprehensively.

"They'll be put back by the time His Lordship wants them," the Housekeeper answered. "Now you enjoy yourself, Miss. I hope I've brought a selection you like."

"I am sure you have," Neoma answered, "and thank you very much."

When the Housekeeper had gone, she looked at the books with interest and found that they showed another side of the Marquis's character which she had not suspected.

Thoughts on the Present Discontents, by Edmund Burke, surprised her, as she had not thought the Marquis would be interested in Politics. The next was *Of Marriage and the Single Life,* by Francis Bacon, and, still more surprisingly, there were also three books of poetry.

She opened a book of William Cowper's poems, which she had read ever since she was a child and had learnt "John Gilpin" to recite to her father and mother.

Turning over the pages, she looked with interest at some of the lines that the Marquis had marked.

She could not imagine him, of all people, liking poetry, and yet he had underlined two lines which she found it difficult to understand:

> *I was a stricken deer, that left the herd*
> *Long since.*

'Why should that apply to him in any way?' she wondered.

It was hard to imagine anyone less stricken or that he had left the herd. He was definitely very much a part of it.

Almost as if she were on a voyage of exploration, she picked up one of the other books and found that it was the poems of Dryden. She thumbed through the pages, finding several old favourites. Then, curious, she opened another volume.

Here again were poems she had herself read and liked, by John Donne, although some, her mother had told her, were written when the poet was a rake.

Again she found that the Marquis had marked certain lines:

> *Wilt thou forgive that sin by which I've won*
> *Others to sin, and made my sin their door?*

"What does that mean to him?" she asked herself.

Could he really be aware that he sinned and involved other people in his sinning? It was impossible to believe!

On another page she found marked:

> *I am two fools, I know*
> *For loving, and for saying so.*

Neoma put down the book and wondered with whom the Marquis had been in love. Had she been very beautiful?

It was difficult to imagine him in love in the way she thought of love: something rapturous, glorious, and sacred because love came from God.

She could see his face so clearly, the contempt in his eyes, the cynical twist of his lips. Yet when they had ridden together he had seemed different—or had that just been her imagination?

The light began to fade and Elsie came in to pull the curtains and light the candles by her bed and also the huge Dresden china candelabra which stood on either side of the dressing-table.

"There is no need for so many lights, Elsie," Neoma said, "candles are expensive."

Elsie laughed.

"That's not something you should say in this house, Miss."

"Why not?"

"Because His Lordship insists on lights in every room, whether they're in use or not."

"In every room?" Neoma repeated in astonishment.

"Yes, Miss, he says he hates darkness and he likes when he comes home to see all the windows in the house shining and not looking black and empty."

"It is the most extraordinary thing I have ever heard!" Neoma exclaimed.

"That's what I thinks, Miss, but if His Lordship can afford it—why shouldn't he have what he wants?"

"Why not indeed?" Neoma said with a smile.

Elsie gave a little sigh, then she said:

"I daresay it sounds queer to you, Miss, having rooms all lit up with nobody in them. But we've got used to it. At least we're never afraid of ghosts and spooky corners!"

"That must certainly be a blessing."

"Good-night, Miss," Elsie said, and walked towards the door. As she reached it, she added:

"Excuse me, Miss, but if I was you I'd lock my door—then you can sleep without being disturbed."

Neoma looked at her in surprise.

Then it suddenly struck her that the maid was warning her against someone like Lord Dadchett! Supposing . . .

Because she was frightened, Neoma quickly jumped out of bed and locked the door to the corridor.

Then she wondered if she should lock the door to Peregrine's room also.

"I am sure nobody will come that way," she told herself.

Feeling safe and secure, she got back into bed and picked up John Donne's poems again.

Now she found several lines thickly scored.

> *And swear*
> *No where*
> *Lives a woman true and fair.*

Neoma read it over several times, then she thought to herself that perhaps this was the clue she had sought in trying to understand the Marquis.

"No where lives a woman true and fair!"

Could that be what he had found in his experience? Could that be why he was so cynical?

She had a feeling that she would never know the answer, and it was somehow depressing.

Finally, as she blew out the candles preparatory to going to sleep, she thought to herself that because he had been kind in saving her from Lord Dadchett, she should pray for him as she prayed for Peregrine and Charles.

It seemed almost an impertinence where the Marquis was concerned because he was so imperious and, as Avril had said, too stiff-necked to need the help of anybody, least of all herself.

And yet the words he had underlined made him seem a little more human.

"No where lives a woman true and fair!"

Who had deceived him and why? And had he later found a woman who was true?

Again it was an unanswerable question, and she fell asleep thinking of the Marquis.

* * *

Neoma awoke with a start to hear someone knocking on the door. For a moment she was afraid of who it might be. Then she realised that it was morning and she knew it must be Elsie.

She got out of bed and opened the door, saying:

"Good-morning, Elsie."

"Good-morning, Miss. I'm sorry if I've woken you up too early, but His Lordship told me to do so."

"His Lordship?" Neoma questioned.

"Yes, Miss. He thought you might like to ride with him and he said to tell you he'd be leaving in half-an-hour."

"I would love to ride with his Lordship!" Neoma exclaimed, her eyes alight.

Elsie crossed the room to draw back the curtains, saying as she did so:

"Mrs. Elverton tells me last night that if there was any question of you a-going riding, Miss, I were to ask you if you'd like to borrow a riding-skirt. There's no jacket to it, but it's hot, so I doubts if you'll need one."

"But of course I would like to borrow one," Neoma replied. "How kind of Mrs. Elverton to think of it!"

She was partially dressed when Elsie returned to the bedroom with a riding-skirt of a thin material in a very attractive shade of blue.

It was slightly too big round the waist, but Elsie sewed her into it, and over a stiff petticoat Neoma knew that it was a far more appropriate garment for riding than was one of her thin gowns.

She fortunately had a muslin blouse which she had made herself, and since she had no hat she arranged her hair into a tight chignon so that it would not blow about.

Then, because the excitement of again riding one of the Marquis's horses was a thrill beyond anything she had ever known, she ran quickly down the stairs.

He was waiting for her in the Hall and she thought that there was a faint smile on his lips as he saw the way she was dressed.

"I am afraid I have no hat," she apologised, "but Mrs. Elverton has lent me a skirt."

"There will be nobody to see you at this hour of the morning," the Marquis replied, "and I thought since you went to bed early you would not mind being wakened early."

As he spoke Neoma looked at him quickly, wondering if he was annoyed with her for not coming down to dinner the preceding night. But she did not wish to question him, and the horses were outside the front door.

He helped her into the saddle, then they were off and it was difficult to think of anything except how exciting it was to be mounted on such a fine thoroughbred, riding in the early morning before anybody else was awake.

They galloped as they had done yesterday, and when at last they slowed their horses down to a walk, the Marquis said:

"I have never seen anyone who was less likely to be suffering from a headache!"

Neoma gave a little laugh.

"I can see, My Lord, that you are determined to extract an apology from me."

"On the contrary, I think you were extremely wise to do what you did," the Marquis replied, "but it was the first time I can remember anybody deliberately evading my hospitality."

Neoma did not reply and he went on:

"But as you had already made it very clear what you thought of the dinner-party the night before, I was not really surprised."

"I am . . . sorry if what I said was . . . rude."

"Not rude," the Marquis replied, "only slightly unpredictable. You are an unusual person, Miss King."

Before Neoma could answer, he added:

"I have just realised that I do not know your other name. What is it?"

"Neoma!"

The Marquis raised his eye-brows, then he said:

" 'Light of the New Moon'! Why should you have been christened that?"

Neoma smiled.

"I suppose I should be surprised that you know ancient Greek, but I am not."

"Why not?"

"Because I read last night some of the books you enjoy, and they are what I have always enjoyed myself."

"I am not quite certain what you are talking about," the Marquis replied.

Neoma suddenly thought that she had been indiscreet, but it was too late to retract.

"If I tell you . . . you will not be . . . annoyed?"

"It depends what I hear."

"Then I would be wise not to tell you."

"I have a feeling you are blackmailing me," the Marquis said, "so I will capitulate and say I will not be annoyed."

"Well, last night when I had dinner in bed," Neoma began, "I asked Mrs. Elverton if I could have some books to read. She told me that you have twenty thousand books in your Library, and I did not think you would miss one."

"What did she bring you?" the Marquis asked.

"She brought me several books which she told me came from your private Sitting-Room, and I particularly enjoyed rereading John Donne, as I have known and loved his poetry for many years."

The Marquis did not speak and Neoma added quickly:

"Please . . . you must not be annoyed with Mrs. Elverton."

"I am not in the least annoyed," the Marquis replied, "I am only surprised. What else did you read?"

"Dryden, and I thought that he was the most predictable poet that I should have expected you to read."

"Why?" the Marquis asked.

For a moment Neoma thought she should not reply, then somehow she could not help teasing him, and she quoted:

> "The God-like hero sat
> On his imperial throne."

For a moment she thought there was a look of anger in the Marquis's eyes, then suddenly he began to laugh.

"Is that how I appear at the end of the Dining-Room table?"

"Exactly!"

Again the Marquis laughed. Then he said:

"You have forgotten how the poem goes on a little later, or perhaps you are warning me."

"Tell me."

> "Fallen from his high estate
> And walt'ring in his blood . . .

> *On the bare earth expos'd he lies,*
> *With not a friend to close his eyes."*

"That will never happen to you," Neoma said.

"I hope not, but you may in some obscure way be seeing with your 'inner eye' just as you saw yesterday that *Diamond* would not win the Derby."

"Were you very . . . upset?"

"I was disappointed."

"Of course, and I am . . . afraid you must have . . . lost a lot of . . . money."

"I never bet on my own horses."

"Surely that is unusual?"

"I believe so, but it is a rule I made long ago. So my only loss was the prize-money, and of course the prestige."

"There are always other years."

"Of course, and are you in fact prophesying that I shall win sometime?"

"I cannot see as far as that," Neoma said, "and anyway, what I . . . felt yesterday, I may never . . . feel again."

"But you have felt such things before?"

"Once or twice."

"I wonder whether if you went racing with the sole intention of making money, it would be possible for you to pick the winner."

Neoma shook her head.

"I am sure it would not work like that."

At the same time, it suddenly struck her that perhaps that would be a way to win the money that Peregrine needed so urgently.

Then she told herself that she was certain it was something that would not happen, and besides, the one thing she must do was to discourage Peregrine from gambling in any form, and that idea would be an incitment she dared not risk.

"What are you thinking about?" the Marquis asked suddenly.

"Gambling."

"It is something you wish to do?"

"No, of course not! I hate it! It is wrong! If people want money, they should work for it in some way, not just win or lose it on the turn of a card!"

She spoke so vehemently that the Marquis said:

"Gambling obviously has a very personal meaning for you. Has Standish been taking chances of which you do not approve?"

This was too near the truth for it to be comfortable, and Neoma said quickly:

"Shall we gallop? I want to feel the wind in my face and feel it blow away the cob-webs."

"I think you are evading my question again," the Marquis remarked.

But already they were moving more quickly and soon the horses were moving at a gallop.

All too quickly the ride seemed to come to an end and they turned for home.

'Soon I must be leaving,' Neoma thought, 'and never again shall I ride such a magnificent horse or indeed with a man who rides so well.'

She looked at the Marquis and thought it would be impossible to imagine that a man could look more at home in the saddle or more part of his horse.

There was an athletic fitness about him which seemed to be echoed by the supremely fit stallion he was riding.

The sun was percolating golden through the branches of the trees, and in the distance the lake seemed to shimmer in the sun.

It was all so beautiful, so compelling in a way she had never known before, and Neoma felt her whole being respond to it.

"I shall always remember this," she said, almost as if she spoke to herself.

She was still looking at Syth, and the Marquis followed the direction of her eyes, then came back to look at her.

"You speak as if it is already in the past."

"That is what it will be . . . tomorrow."

"And you would like to prevent that from happening?"

She gave him a child-like smile.

"It is . . . like a beautiful dream and one wants to go on dreaming forever because it is so . . . perfect and part of another world . . . and yet at the same time one knows that it is inevitable . . . that one must wake up to . . . reality."

As she spoke, she told herself that what she was seeing was a dream, a mirage, something that would vanish, and she would waken to the horror of knowing that Peregrine could not pay what was owed and neither could Charles.

'I will try not to think about it as we ride home,' she thought to herself.

But it was too late.

The difficulties ahead were already in her mind, and now there was only today in which to find the IOU and extract themselves from the unhappiness and despair of a menacing future.

She was suddenly aware that the Marquis was watching her face and after a moment he asked:

"What is troubling you?"

"Waking up," she replied. "My dream has . . . vanished, I can no longer hold it."

"That happens to all of us," the Marquis said cynically.

Neoma glanced at him uncertainly.

She suddenly wanted to tell him the truth and ask him to understand. Then she knew it would betray Peregrine and they would be worse off than they were already.

She looked at Syth and thought despairingly how little two thousand pounds meant to its owner.

Candles alight in every room, golden ornaments on the Dining-Room table, expensive wine poured down the throats of those who did not appreciate it, and every room filled with treasures worth a fortune.

And in contrast, Peregrine, penniless, possessing only an unsaleable and dilapidated house, and yet bound by an unwritten code to beggar himself for a man who had no need of his money.

The horses began to move more quickly and as

they went it seemed to Neoma that their hoofs repeated over and over again:

"A debt of honour ... of honour ... of honour ... !"

Chapter Five

When they reached the house Neoma went quickly upstairs to her bedroom to change her riding-skirt.

Elsie was buttoning her into a thin gown in which she intended to go to the races when there was a knock on the door.

Neoma realised that it was the communicating-door between her room and Peregrine's, and as she said: "Come in!" she wondered how she could indicate to Elsie that she wished to be alone.

Fortunately, the maid was well versed in such situations, for as Peregrine entered, she picked up Neoma's discarded riding-skirt and went out into the corridor.

Peregrine waited until the door had closed behind her before he said:

"I have to see you alone. Our plans have changed."

"Changed?" Neoma questioned.

"Yes," he replied. "Last night Sir Edmund Courtenay asked Charles and me to stay with him."

He realised that his sister was curious, and he explained:

"Sir Edmund is an extremely keen pugilist, and he is staging a Mill at his house at Hatfield."

There was an eager note in Peregrine's voice as he continued:

"It is between two famous champions, and you can imagine how exciting it will be."

Neoma knew that Peregrine had always been interested in Prize-Fighting, although because her mother could not bear the thought of men striking each other with their bare fists, he had never been allowed to box.

"I can understand your wanting to go, dearest," she said, "but are you saying we must leave here earlier?"

"We leave this evening," Peregrine said, "after the racing."

He gave a little laugh as he said:

"I do not expect you will mind missing dinner! Last night the behaviour of the women was even worse than it was the night before."

Neoma wanted to say that she thought that would be impossible, but instead she asked:

"What time are we leaving?"

"As soon as we return from the Downs," Peregrine answered. "I should imagine that if the Marquis leaves after the big race, as he is sure to do, it will be just before five o'clock."

"What about the carriage you ordered?"

"Courtenay says he will take us all to London in his Cabriolet," Peregrine replied. "Then Charles and I will be travelling to Hatfield with him early tomorrow morning, and as this is a bachelor-party there is no question of you being invited."

Neoma felt that that was a relief, but she saw by Peregrine's expression that he had something more to say to her.

"What is it?" she asked.

Peregrine glanced over his shoulder as if afraid somebody might be listening, then said in a low voice:

"This is our opportunity!"

"What do you mean?"

"As you had a headache last night, you can easily say that you are not well enough to go to the races today."

Neoma waited apprehensively, her eyes on his face.

"Charles has discovered where the Marquis keeps

his money—at least his loose change—and that is undoubtedly where my IOU will be."

"How did Charles find that out?" Neoma enquired.

"Courtenay asked the Marquis to cash a cheque
for him so that he could go on gambling and Charles
wanted to do the same."

Neoma gave a little cry.

"He is not gambling again and losing money?"

"As a matter of fact, he had won by the end of
the evening," Peregrine said, "but I told him before he
started that it was a silly thing to do."

"I should certainly think it was!" Neoma said indignantly. "How can he be so reckless? He might have
lost everything we won at the races."

"That is what I told him," Peregrine replied, "but,
needless to say, the Marquis's good wines are too strong
for his head, and mine too if it comes to that."

"Oh, Peregrine, how can you both be so foolish?" Neoma asked.

At the same time, she felt that it was extremely
reprehensible of the Marquis to give men as young as
Peregrine and Charles so much to drink and then encourage them to gamble.

She found herself remembering the lines he had
marked of John Donne's:

> *Will thou forgive that sin by which I've won*
> *Others to sin, and made my sin their door?*

That is exactly what he had done, she thought
furiously, with his dissolute parties and the endless
drinking followed up by gambling.

'I hate him,' she thought to herself.

Then she thought of him riding beside her, the
way he had handled his horse, and it was difficult to
believe that what she had told herself was entirely
true.

"Go on with what you were telling me," she said
to Peregrine.

"The Marquis took Courtenay and Charles to
his Sitting-Room, which is in his Suite on this
floor."

'That is where his books came from last night,' Neoma thought.

As if she already anticipated what Peregrine was going to ask her, she stiffened.

"If you are here in the house alone," he went on, "and we are at the races, all you have to do is to slip along the corridor and look in his desk. Charles said the money was loose in the middle drawer."

There was silence. Then Neoma asked:

"How can you . . . ask me to do such a . . . thing? How can I . . . steal from the Marquis?"

"It has to be done!" Peregrine replied. "You know that I have only three days left in which to find the two thousand pounds. For Heaven's sake, Neoma, how else can I find such a sum?"

"I know . . . I know!" she said miserably. "But to steal from a man who has shown us . . . nothing but kindness in his own way seems . . . utterly and completely . . . despicable."

Peregrine turned to walk across the room, then stood at the window looking out onto the Park."

"Two thousand pounds means nothing to the Marquis," he said. "If I cannot find it and he will not accept the Manor as payment for the debt, I shall go to the Fleet."

"The debtors' prison?" Neoma cried. "No-one, not even the Marquis, could treat you like that!"

"I am quite certain it would not trouble him in the slightest," Peregrine said in a bitter voice. "Anyway, even if I were not imprisoned, I should have to resign from White's. No other Club would have me, and what do you imagine I shall do with myself in such circumstances?"

There was no answer to this question and Neoma thought despairingly that he was pushing her into a corner where she would have to do what he wanted because it was the only way she could save him.

She drew a deep breath and said in a voice he could barely hear:

"Tell me . . . again where Charles . . . saw the money."

*   *   *

There were few people downstairs when Neoma and Peregrine went into the Breakast-Room and those who were there looked as if they had passed a bad night and were definitely suffering from the aftermath.

Neoma ate quickly, too worried about what lay ahead of her to feel hungry as she had the preceding morning.

As she and Peregrine walked towards the Hall he said to her in a low voice:

"I am grateful, you know I am! Only for God's sake do not get caught, or we will be in a worse position than we are at the moment."

"I will be careful," Neoma promised.

Only as she reached the Hall did she know that someone had to tell the Marquis that she would not be joining the party going to the race-course, and she thought it only poetic justice that it should be Peregrine.

It would be impossible after they had been riding together to say that she still had a headache. She thought that perhaps he would suppose that she had no desire to mix further with the women whom he knew she despised, preferring her own company and perhaps a chance to read.

It was then, after having instructed Peregrine what to say, that she thought as she went upstairs to her room that it was providential that Mrs. Elverton had brought her the Marquis's books the night before.

She could take them back to his private Sitting-Room, and if anyone saw her, that would be her excuse for being in his part of the house.

At the same time, she felt her heart give a nervous contraction at the idea not only of stealing from the Marquis but even of entering his private Suite.

However, she realised that she had a long time to wait before it would be possible to avoid being seen by the innumerable servants who appeared to be everywhere.

As soon as she heard the sound of a horn being blown as the coach went down the drive, she ran down the stairs in search of Mr. Greystone.

Before she left her bedroom she received another piece of information that was helpful.

"Aren't you going to the races, Miss?" Elsie asked when Neoma made no effort to put on her bonnet, which had been laid out for her on a chair.

"No, Elsie," Neoma replied. "I think it would be too tiring, as I am returning to London tonight instead of tomorrow morning."

"I thought you'd be doing that, Miss," Elsie said. "When you'd gone down to breakfast, Mr. Standish's valet told me he wanted his trunk packed by five o'clock."

"And mine must be ready at the same time."

"It won't take me long, Miss," Elsie said. "You've not half as much to pack as the other ladies."

Neoma did not answer and the maid went on:

"I've got some jobs to do this morning for Mrs. Elverton, but I'll pack immediately after our dinner, and everything'll be ready for you, Miss. I'll just leave out your travelling-gown, so's you can change at the last moment."

"Thank you," Neoma said. Then she asked:

"What time do you have your meal?"

"It's usually at noon, Miss, but when the Master's not at home we has it later, as that's what the kitchen prefers."

"How late?"

"One o'clock, Miss, but I'll be up here by two, so don't worry that your trunk won't be ready."

"I am sure it will be," Neoma said with a smile, knowing that she had found out what she wanted to know.

"If I have time in the afternoon I would like to see the gardens," she said. "I wonder if you would be kind enough to ask if I could have luncheon at half-after-twelve?"

"I'll do that, Miss, and I expect you'd like to have it in the little Dining-Room as you'll be alone."

"That would be very nice," Neoma replied, then hurried to find Mr. Greystone.

She spent the morning seeing wonderful rooms in

the house which left her almost speechless at their beauty.

The pictures and the china in the State-Rooms alone made her feel that she could spend years looking at them and never be satiated.

The Library was all that Mrs. Elverton had said it was, long and high, its ceiling painted by Verrio.

Mr. Greystone told her that the huge mahogany writing-table had been designed by the famous William Kent for the Third Marquis.

Neoma enjoyed seeing the large Dining-Room when it was not filled with people and she had the chance to admire the Van Dykes on the walls and the gilt side-tables with their marble tops.

It was past twelve o'clock before Mr. Greystone said:

"I am afraid, Miss King, I have an appointment with His Lordship's Agent in five minutes. Perhaps if you have nothing better to do after luncheon I could show you a few more rooms."

"You know I would love that," Neoma replied, "and thank you for all you have shown me this morning. It is impossible for me to express how much I admire this wonderful house."

"It has given me great pleasure to show it to someone so appreciative," Mr. Greystone replied, "and I shall be disappointed if you leave before you have seen everything."

"So shall I," Neoma answered. "May I come to your office at about two o'clock?"

"I shall be waiting for you," Mr. Greystone promised.

He left her and Neoma went to the Salon and waited to be told that her luncheon was ready.

She was not hungry because although the food was delicious she kept thinking of what she had to do, and she felt that every nerve in her body rebelled against it.

But she knew that to save Peregrine she would have done much worse things, and however much it was against her principles to steal, she had no choice but to agree to what he had asked of her.

She finished luncheon and because she was listening for it she heard a bell ring far away in the distance which meant that the servants would all troop towards the East Wing.

During her tour with Mr. Greystone, Neoma had seen a plan of the house, and she knew exactly where the King's Room, which was where the Marquis slept, was situated.

It had been given the name after George II had stayed at Syth, and as he had been accompanied by his wife, the Queen's Room was adjacent to the one used by the Marquis.

Neoma could not help wondering whether this room was now occupied by Vicky Vale as she was the Marquis's particular guest.

It seemed strange, she thought, that the gentlemen and the ladies they had brought with them were put in rooms side-by-side.

Neoma remembered that at home when they had a house-party, her mother had always arranged that the bachelors should sleep in one part of the house and the unmarried women in another.

But she supposed that people who knew each other well liked to be together and she was certainly glad that Peregrine's room had been next door to hers.

She went upstairs, looked into her own bedroom, and found, as she had expected, that Elsie was not there.

Then with a hand that was trembling despite her resolution to be calm and courageous, she picked up two of the books that Mrs. Elverton had brought her, one by Edmund Burke and the other by Francis Bacon.

With her heart beating so loudly that she thought if anyone had been about they would have heard it, she walked down the long corridor which led past the State-Rooms and on to where at the very end of the centre block the King's Suite was situated.

For a moment she wondered if perhaps when the Marquis was away his valet kept the rooms locked.

Then she knew it was very unlikely that anything of the sort would be done in a house where they would not expect there to be thieves and robbers, especially amongst the Marquis's guests.

Very, very cautiously she opened the door of the room that she was sure, from what she had seen on the plan, was the Marquis's Sitting-Room.

She was right, and she saw as she entered the room, quickly shutting the door behind her, that it was just as magnificent as she might have expected it to be.

In the centre of the room there was a huge desk, flat-topped with elaborate gilt handles and gilt feet.

There were a number of book-cases and some exquisite pieces of furniture that Neoma at any other time would have stopped to admire.

But she was intent on only one thing—to find the IOU which could ruin completely and irrevocably Peregrine's life forever.

She set the books down on the writing-desk and slowly, because she was frightened by what she was doing, pulled open the middle drawer.

As Peregrine had told her, there was quite a number of sovereigns lying loose inside it, amongst a number of note-books, several pens, and other small objects.

By opening the drawer wider Neoma saw that besides the sovereigns there were two cheques.

She saw Sir Edmund Courtenay's signature on one and Charles's on the other.

She pushed them to one side, putting her hand farther into the drawer.

She felt a piece of paper and hoped it was what she sought, but when she pulled it out, it only contained some notes referring to the breeding of a horse.

Now she began to feel frantically that despite Peregrine's expectations, what she sought was not there.

She turned over the note-books, thinking that perhaps the IOU might be underneath, and as she did so, she remembered that there would be not only Peregrine's IOU but also a number from the other Members of White's who had been playing the night Charles had won and lost a fortune.

She found several sovereigns which had become separated from the rest, and three silver crowns, which her father had always said were a nuisance because they were so heavy to carry.

'It must be here! It must be here somewhere!' Neoma thought.

Although she searched the drawer very thoroughly, there was no sign of an IOU of any sort.

It struck her that perhaps the Marquis had put them all together in another drawer, and because Peregrine had said he was always winning, perhaps he had a great pile of debts owed by the unfortunate men he fleeced.

Leaving the middle drawer open, as if she thought that by some miracle the IOU would materialise there, she pulled open the top drawer on the right-hand side, to find that it contained only writing-paper and quill pens.

She closed it and, going down on her knees, opened the next drawer.

Here again she was disappointed. It contained leather-bound books, most of them embossed with the Marquis's crest.

Despairingly Neoma opened the bottom drawer.

Here, she thought, must be the papers she sought.

There were a number of documents tied together which looked as if they might be deeds or perhaps bills.

There were also some letters, and she moved everything in the drawer to try to find what she sought.

Suddenly a voice asked:

"Could I perhaps be of assistance?"

If a pistol had been fired by her ear Neoma could not have been more startled or more shocked.

For a moment she was frozen into immobility.

She was well aware who had spoken, and she wished that the floor could open up and swallow her, or that she could die.

"I am interested to know why my possessions should concern you," the Marquis said in the cold, sarcastic voice that she had heard him use when she first arrived at Syth.

Because she had held her breath for so long at the first shock of knowing that he was behind her, Neoma found herself giving an audible gasp before, with what entailed a superhuman effort, she rose to her feet.

It is always said that a drowning man sees his whole life pass before him before he dies, and she thought that the opened middle drawer of the desk, with the gold coins shining in it, and the drawer in which she had just been searching would be imprinted on her mind forever.

"If it is money you want," the Marquis said, "I imagine you have not had time to help yourself to what is lying there."

He moved as he spoke, and now he was standing in front of her and she felt that she was compelled to raise her eyes to his.

"I . . . I was not . . . taking y-your . . . money," she managed to say, but even as she spoke, she knew it was not true.

It was money she was stealing, although it was merely "paper money"—money that existed only in Peregrine's imagination.

"I presume I am entitled to an explanation?" the Marquis suggested.

Neoma looked away from him and again at the open drawers.

She would have to tell him the truth, she knew. What else could she do?

"I . . . I will . . . explain . . . what I was . . . d-doing," she said, "if . . . if you . . . promise to . . . believe me."

"I hardly think you are in a position to make conditions," the Marquis answered. "But shall I say that unless you strain my credulity too far, I shall try to believe you."

As he spoke he walked towards the mantelpiece and when he reached it he turned round to say:

"I suppose what you are doing must have been well planned. Was it Standish's idea or yours?"

There was a harshness in his voice that made Neoma shudder.

Then, perhaps because she looked lost and forlorn standing still beside the open drawers of the desk, the Marquis said:

"Suppose you come and sit down while I listen to your explanation, and before I take any action."

"A-action?" Neoma questioned.

"There are quite stringent penalties inflicted by the Courts for stealing and even attempting to steal."

As he spoke, she had the feeling that he suspected she had already put some sovereigns in a concealed pocket.

Because the idea was so horrifying, she moved towards him and said:

"Please . . . please . . . listen to me."

"I am prepared to do so," the Marquis answered, "so sit down."

He indicated a chair beside the fireplace and Neoma sank down in it, feeling that if she had not done so her legs would no longer have supported her.

"The . . . the night you . . . won all the money at White's Club from . . . Charles . . ." she began in a faltering little voice.

"Waddesdon? Is he in this too?" the Marquis enquired. "I thought that you and Standish were working alone."

"It all happened," Neoma answered, "because you . . . won so much . . . money from Charles when he had had . . . too much to drink."

"What has that to do with it?" the Marquis enquired.

"Do you really think he could have . . . played in that . . . reckless . . . ridiculous manner . . . if he had not been . . . drunk?" Neoma asked.

For one moment the anger she had felt when Peregrine had told her that the Marquis had been well aware of Charles's condition came back to her, and she said in a very different tone from the one in which she had been speaking:

"Charles did not know what he was doing. He would not have gambled at all if he had been in his senses, for the simple reason that . . . he has no money!"

The Marquis did not speak and she went on:

"The same applies to Peregrine. They have hardly enough to live in London, let alone gamble at the Club or anywhere else!"

"Then they should not do so."

"They never do as a rule, but the night you won six thousand pounds from Charles, they had been given a great deal to drink and he was living in a fantasy-world where he believed himself to be rich and had no idea what he was actually doing."

"A very plausible explanation!" the Marquis said sneeringly.

Neoma looked at him and felt as if she could not go on.

Whatever she said, he was obviously not going to believe her, and she thought that if she had any pride she would go from the room and leave him to think what he liked.

Then she remembered Peregrine and what it would mean to him.

The Marquis must have seen her indecision and what she was feeling, from the expression in her eyes, because after a moment he said in a kinder tone:

"Go on!"

"Would you . . . please . . . sit down?" Neoma asked. "You are . . . so tall and it . . . frightens me more than I am . . . already when you are . . . towering over me."

"So you are frightened," the Marquis remarked. "Is this your first adventure in crime?"

"Of course it is!" Neoma said angrily. "Do you imagine that I would . . . ?"

She stopped suddenly and said:

"Please . . . let me finish . . . my story . . . then you can . . . judge for yourself . . . if what I have tried to do is so very . . . wrong."

The Marquis did not speak and after a moment she said quickly:

"Charles and Peregrine have been friends for a very long time . . . and they have played games as if they were . . . rich. At White's that night they played Piquet together and, because they thought the other Members of the Club would laugh at them or think it strange that they played for nothing, they made pretended bets on the cards and lost and won entirely imaginary sums to each other, for which they wrote out fictitious IOUs."

She glanced at the Marquis and saw by the sudden alert look in his eyes that he had already guessed what she was about to say.

"When you won six thousand pounds from Charles," she said, "two thousand pounds of what he paid you was a fictitious IOU to him from Peregrine."

She felt as if her voice echoed round the room.

There was a pause before the Marquis said:

"What you are saying is that Standish cannot meet his obligations!"

"Of course he cannot!" Neoma replied. "He has not even twenty pounds at the moment, let alone two thousand! But he says it is a debt of honour and you will expect to be paid in . . . three days' . . . time!"

Her voice trembled on the last words.

"If he defaults," the Marquis said slowly, "what does he expect to happen?"

"You know what he expects!" Neoma answered. "If you press him he will go to the Fleet prison. If you merely admit it is a bad debt, then he will have to resign from his Club and be ostracised by . . . everybody in the . . . Sporting World."

She clasped her hands together.

"Oh . . . please . . . please . . . do not do that to him. What would he have left? What would he . . . do?"

"It means so much to you?" the Marquis asked unexpectedly.

"It means . . . more than I can . . . explain . . . it means everything!"

She was just about to add: "Because he is my brother," when she remembered how Charles had warned her that if anyone knew that Peregrine had taken his sister to stay at Syth, he would be criticised in no uncertain fashion.

Whatever else she thought they could not salvage from the wreck of their plans, she must save Peregrine from that.

Aloud she said:

"Peregrine has been very . . . kind to me. I wanted to help him, and I felt that if I stole the IOU, you might not . . . notice it had gone."

"I might not have done so," the Marquis admitted, "but my Comptroller, who is in London and deals with such things, would undoubtedly have been aware that I had been defrauded."

Neoma looked at him, a startled expression in her eyes.

"You mean . . . the IOU is not . . . here?"

"No," the Marquis replied. "When I have been gambling my Comptroller sees to everything, including what you call the 'debts of honour' I am owed."

It was what she might have expected, Neoma thought, and what Peregrine and Charles should have realised before they got her into this uncomfortable position.

The Marquis's eyes were on her face and after a moment she asked:

"Wh-what are you . . . going to do?"

"I was just asking myself the same question," the Marquis answered.

Because it suddenly struck her that it was strange that he should be there, she asked:

"Why did you . . . come back?"

"Because Standish told me that you thought the racing would be too much for you as you were leaving this evening, and I returned so that we could have luncheon together."

Neoma looked at him in astonishment and he went on:

"I thought too it would be your last opportunity of looking over the stables. If my memory is right, you have only inspected half my horses."

"I want to see the others," Neoma murmured, "but there has never been time."

It flashed through her mind that whatever happened in the future, she would always remember their rides together and the magnificence of his horses.

"You can imagine," the Marquis said, "that it was somewhat of a surprise on my return to find you not reading John Donne, as I expected you to be doing, but rifling my private desk."

"I . . . I have tried to . . . explain why I was . . . doing it," Neoma said unhappily.

Then suddenly, impulsively, without even thinking what she was doing, she rose from the chair and crossed the hearth to kneel down at the Marquis's side.

"Please . . ." she begged, "please do not make . . . Peregrine pay you the . . . two thousand pounds. The only thing he possesses is his home in the . . . country. He cannot find a . . . purchaser and he does not think it is even worth the money he owes you . . . but he can give you the . . . deed to it. But when it is gone . . . he will have nothing in the future . . . but the clothes he stands up in."

Her eyes searched the Marquis's face and she thought that he was looking as Avril had described him, disdainful and contemptuous.

"Please be kind. I know you have been . . . hurt and disillusioned . . ."

"Who told you I had been hurt and disillusioned?" the Marquis interrupted.

"I was sure of it when I read what you had marked in the poems of John Donne."

"If I marked them," the Marquis said coldly, "I did so many years ago, so they certainly do not apply today."

"If you marked them when you were young," Neoma said, "then you will remember that Peregrine is very young too? He is only nineteen."

"As young as that?" the Marquis exclaimed.

"Yes, as young as that," Neoma said. "When one is young one does a lot of stupid things which one may regret later."

There was silence, then the Marquis said slowly:

"As I see it, it is not really Standish who owes me the money, but Charles Waddesdon."

"He cannot pay either," Neoma said. "In fact he is almost in a worse state than Peregrine, for the simple reason that he is in debt."

"It seems to me that these two young men should have something better to do than play with fire."

"That is what I think," Neoma said, "but . . ."

Again she stopped herself when she was just going to explain why neither of them could afford to go to Oxford and they had no money with which to buy themselves into a decent Regiment.

There was no other occupation open for gentlemen, or if there was, she had never heard of it.

Then she thought that it would show too close an intimacy with Peregrine if she said very much more, so instead she merely said:

"Whatever you may feel about them . . . please be merciful."

The Marquis looked at her in what she thought was a strangely searching manner. Then unexpectedly he rose to his feet, leaving her still kneeling beside the chair.

"I have a proposition to put to you," he said, "and I want you to consider it very carefully."

"Yes . . . of course," Neoma said nervously, afraid of what he was about to suggest.

"I expect that you are well aware of my reputation," the Marquis said, "that I am hard and ruthless, and I have never been known to do a kind act."

Neoma looked at him in surprise. It was certainly what had been said about him, but she did not expect him to know it.

As if she had spoken aloud, he said with a mocking smile:

"I am well aware of what is said about me, and let me assure you that everything is true and the way I wish it to be."

"But why . . . why?" Neoma questioned.

"I am not talking about myself, but you."

"Me?"

"If, as you say," the Marquis said, "you are prepared to do anything to help Standish and his equally foolish friend, Waddesdon, then my suggestion may meet with your approval."

"What . . . is it?"

She had a feeling that it was going to be something frightening and her question was hardly above a whisper.

"I will cancel Standish's debt," the Marquis said, "or, if you wish, let him believe that you have stolen it from me and that I am so half-witted as not to be aware of it."

There was a scathing note in his voice which made Neoma feel uncomfortable as he went on:

"In return, you will come and stay with me here at Syth after the house-party has left tomorrow morning."

For a moment Neoma felt that she could not have heard him aright.

"S-stay . . . with you . . . here?"

"Why not?" he enquired. "I am sure you will find plenty to interest you in my horses, if not in me."

"You want me to . . . stay . . . alone?"

"I was not suggesting that anyone should accompany you," the Marquis said drily.

"B-but . . . for how long?"

He made a gesture with his hand.

"I am prepared to leave that to you."

It suddenly struck Neoma that she could do as he asked, because Peregrine would be away and therefore would not be aware that she had left the house.

He had said that he was leaving London early tomorrow morning. She could therefore come back to Syth, if that was what the Marquis wanted, and be home again on Sunday before Peregrine returned.

Even as she thought of it, she told herself that the whole idea was crazy. Why should the Marquis want her to stay at Syth? She was quite certain that Peregrine would be horrified at the idea.

But Peregrine would not know.

It was almost as if a voice within herself argued the pros and cons of the idea, but more important than anything else was the fact that if she did as the Marquis said, he would cancel Peregrine's debt.

She was so bewildered, finding it so difficult to understand why he was asking her to stay, that her mind could only revert to the source of the whole situation.

"How," she asked, "if Peregrine's IOU is in London, can I have stolen it from you here?"

The Marquis smiled, although it was little more than a twist of his lips.

"I imagine we could forge Standish's signature sufficiently well for him not to be suspicious."

"Yes ... of course," Neoma said. "I know exactly how he signs his name, and besides, he had had a lot to drink that particular evening."

"Very well," the Marquis said. "We will set about this nefarious deed, and I presume, before I do so, that you have accepted my proposition?"

"I ... cannot think why you should ... want me," Neoma faltered, "but it would be ... wonderful to have another chance of riding with you."

"It is something I too shall look forward to."

The Marquis walked towards his desk as he spoke and Neoma rose to her feet.

She thought he looked down at the sovereigns in the middle drawer in a suspicious manner, and she said quickly:

"You do not really ... think that I would ... steal money from you?"

He sat down at the desk, then looked up at her and she thought he was challenging her to admit that two thousand pounds was money.

"What you won was ... fairy-gold," she said, "and you know that if it is touched by human hands ... it vanishes."

"Perhaps that is what you will do."

His words made her think of Lord Dadchett and she gave a little shudder. Then she realised that the Marquis was watching her, and she said:

"I was thinking of Lord Dadchett. You will not ... give him my address ... in London ... in case he should try to ... see me?"

"As it happens, I do not know your address,"

the Marquis answered, "and of course I would not let him know where you were, and certainly not that you were returning here."

"He is horrible ... and he frightens me," Neoma said. "That is the main reason why I did not ... wish to come down to dinner last night."

The Marquis did not reply. He merely opened a drawer of his desk and took out a piece of paper.

He tore it into what Neoma thought must be the right size of the IOUs that were used by Members of the Club. Then he passed it to her.

"How big will the IOU be?" she asked.

"Rather large," the Marquis replied, "with his signature beneath it."

Peregrine's signature had always been easy to copy, and Neoma deliberately wrote in a rather unsteady hand as she thought he would have done because like Charles he had been "foxed."

The Marquis looked at it critically.

"I should think that would pass muster," he said, "and if you will take my advice, having shown it to Standish you will tear it up at once."

"That is exactly what I shall do," Neoma agreed, "and thank you, thank you very much for being so kind."

"I think we must discuss my kindness on another occasion," the Marquis replied. "For the moment, I hope I have taken away that look of worry that I have seen on your face ever since you came here."

"It has been terribly worrying, wondering what to do," Neoma admitted, "and I was afraid that one of us might be caught ... just as you caught ... me."

"I think I have told you ever since we met," the Marquis said, "that you are very unpredictable."

"I will ... try not to be now," Neoma replied, "but there are such a lot of things here at Syth that are different from anything I have known before."

"That has been obvious."

From the way he spoke, she was not certain if he was pleased or annoyed.

Holding the IOU in her hand, she looked at him anxiously. Then she asked:

"What do you want me to do now? Mr. Greystone promised to show me more of the house."

The Marquis glanced towards the window.

"As it is such a warm day," he said, "and I have no wish to be indoors, shall we walk in the garden?"

"I would like that," Neoma said, "and ... please ... I want to say again how very ... very grateful I am."

"Perhaps you will express your gratitude tomorrow when we are alone," the Marquis said.

It seemed a strange thing to say, and Neoma looked at him in perplexity, but he continued:

"You have not yet given me your address or told me what time you will be ready for me to collect you."

"Number Six, Royal Avenue."

The Marquis had taken up his pen to write it down. Now he looked up at her with a smile.

"That is strange," he said; "I happen to own the house next door."

"The house next door?" Neoma echoed. "But why? What would you want with a small house like that?"

"For the same reason that Cosmo Blake owns Number Six."

"The man who owns the house in which I am now living gave it to an actress," Neoma said, "but for some reason which I have not been able to ascertain, she quarrelled with him and moved away to a much better part of London—at least, that is what I have been told."

"It sounds very likely," the Marquis said, "but I suggest you have a look at Number Seven and see if you like it better."

"I doubt if I would like any house in London," Neoma answered. "I love the country and never want to be anywhere else. That is why, even though it has been strange and sometimes rather shocking staying here, I have liked being at Syth ... especially when I was riding with you."

"That is certainly something we will do again,"

the Marquis said. "Now let us go into the garden, and I will pick you up from Royal Avenue if you will be ready at eleven o'clock tomorrow morning."

"I will be ready," Neoma answered, "but you will not . . . mention it to . . . Peregrine?"

She spoke anxiously and she thought the Marquis looked at her strangely before he said:

"You do not intend to tell him?"

"No, of course not. If he knew . . . he might . . . forbid me to come."

"And you would obey him?"

Neoma was about to say that she would have to do what Peregrine wanted. Then she thought that it might sound strange.

"I would not . . . wish to . . . upset him," she said rather lamely.

"No, of course not," the Marquis agreed. "It is always a good idea to 'keep all your options open.'"

She did not understand what he meant, but she thought it best not to ask.

"Shall I just put this in my bedroom?" she asked, looking down at the IOU, "and get my bonnet?"

"I should certainly put the IOU in a safe place," the Marquis agreed, "but unless you particularly want something on your head, I like seeing your hair in the sunshine."

She gave him a quick glance of surprise, for it sounded almost as if he had paid her a compliment.

But the Marquis was throwing into the waste-basket the piece of paper from which he had torn the IOU, and he was not looking at her.

"I will be very quick," she said, "and meet you in the Hall."

Chapter Six

Moving through the London traffic, Neoma could not help feeling that it was very exciting to be driving beside the Marquis.

She had never been in a high-perched Phaeton before and she felt as if she had been taken high in the air, out of her ordinary existence and into a different, fantastic world.

But that was what she had felt from the start when she was in contact with the Marquis or his possessions.

Everything about him was divorced completely from the commonplace or the mundane, and as she stole a glimpse at him from under her eye-lashes she thought that he looked more magnificent and even more imperious than usual.

The four chestnuts he was driving were superlative and his Phaeton, painted black and yellow, which were also his racing-colours, was so smart with its silver lamps and silver-crested harness that Neoma told herself that she was in contrast very much the beggarmaid.

Nevertheless she had stayed up late, pressing her gown with its pink ribbons, and she knew that within her limited means she looked as attractive as she could.

When she heard the knock on the door and opened it to see the Marquis outside with his groom holding a team of superlative horses, she felt as if some genie she had conjured up from a fantasy-world had brought her a coach in which to carry her to the Ball.

She also felt somewhat shy, especially as the Marquis, without being invited, walked past her and into the small house.

He looked round the narrow Hall, then to Neoma's surprise glanced into the small Dining-Room in the front of the house and the Sitting-Room at the back.

She felt, without seeing the expression in his eyes, that he was contemptuous of the furniture and the curtains, and although she had arranged everything as comfortably as possible, she knew how inadequate and squalid it must appear to the owner of Syth.

The Marquis, however, did not say anything. He merely asked:

"You are ready?"

Neoma nodded.

She somehow did not trust her voice at that moment.

The Marquis helped her into the Phaeton and his groom collected her trunk to strap it on the back.

Then he turned the horses into the King's Road and drove off.

When she had arrived back in Royal Avenue late last night, Neoma had found it difficult to believe that the Marquis had really invited her to stay at Syth, or rather had compelled her to do so in exchange for the IOU.

She had not been able to tell Peregrine that she had it in her possession until they had reached London and Sir Edmund Courtenay had dropped her and Peregrine at Royal Avenue.

Only when Charles and Avril had said good-bye and Charles had left, saying to Peregrine: "I will see you tomorrow morning at nine o'clock," did Peregrine look at his sister with the question in his eyes which she knew had been trembling on his lips ever since they had left Syth.

"Have you got it?"

There was a note of anxiety in his voice which made her glad that she could reply:

"Yes, it is here!"

As she spoke, she drew the IOU from the reticule she carried on her wrist.

For a moment Peregrine stared at it incredulously, then he flung his arms round her and said:

"You clever, wonderful girl! How did you find it? Oh, Neoma, how can I thank you?"

She had thought it would be difficult to lie to Peregrine and pretend that she had found it in the desk as he had suggested, but because she was so touched by his gratitude and the inexpressible relief in his voice, it was easy to say:

"You were quite right; and now that you are safe, dearest, you must promise me you will never gamble again."

"I will certainly never do anything so stupid as to lose two thousand pounds," Peregrine replied.

He took his arms from her and put his hand to his forehead, saying:

"I can hardly credit that I have no longer to lie awake at night in terror, thinking that we must lose the Manor."

"Go to bed and forget all about it," Neoma said. "I think the best thing we can do is to burn this IOU. It has caused enough trouble as it is."

She hoped Peregrine would agree, but instead he reached out and took the IOU from her hand and said:

"We really ought to frame it so that it will always remind me never to do anything so stupid another time."

"I think you will remember without having to keep that unfortunate piece of paper."

Peregrine stared at his own signature and she watched him anxiously, but he did not say anything, only tore the IOU into small pieces and threw them up into the air.

"I am free!" he said exultantly. "Free, Neoma, and it is all due to you!"

Neoma started to climb the stairs.

"I am tired," she said. "I am going to bed, but

first I had better see that you have a fresh cravat to put on tomorrow morning. Then there will be no need to unpack your trunk as you will be taking it away so early."

She thought as she spoke that the same applied to her own luggage, but she knew that her gown must be pressed and also the ribbons on her bonnet, which she had tied under her chin.

"I shall want at least three cravats," Peregrine announced, "in case I ruin one."

"Not if I tie it for you," Neoma answered.

Nevertheless, she found three and laid them ready in his bedroom.

She did not sleep well, finding herself thinking all the time how strange it was of the Marquis to ask her to go back to Syth and stay with him alone.

Then she told herself that it might have something to do with his horses.

After all, having seen how she could control *Victorious* and being aware of her strange prediction that *Diamond* would not win the Derby, he might easily want her opinion on the other animals he possessed.

"It will be wonderful to ride with him again," she whispered to herself in the darkness.

Because she wanted to have the chance not only of riding on Saturday but also on Sunday morning, she questioned Peregrine closely before he left as to what time he was likely to return.

"I have no idea," he replied carelessly, "not early in the day, at any rate. Sir Edmund is certain to have a dinner-party on Saturday night after the Mill."

"Please do not drink too much," Neoma pleaded. "You know it will make you feel ill."

"I cannot make a spectacle of myself in front of the others," Peregrine replied, "and if you go on nagging at me I will end up with a Prayer-Book in my hand, preaching temperance!"

Neoma laughed because it was such an impossible picture and Peregrine laughed too, and then he put his arm round her and hugged her.

"If it was not for you," he said, "I should be so

sunk in despair that I doubt if I would have been able to watch the Mill. As it is, I shall enjoy every minute."

As he left at nine o'clock when Charles called for him to take him to Sir Edmund's house in Park Lane, Peregrine said:

"I will be back on Sunday in time for dinner at any rate, so have something decent to eat so that Charles can dine with us."

"I would like that," Charles said, "if it is no trouble for Neoma."

She smiled at him.

"You know I would like you to stay. And as Peregrine says, I will try to find something 'decent' to eat."

It was typical that Peregrine did not give her any money to buy what he required, but fortunately she had some left from the two guineas he had given her to spend before they had gone to Syth.

She waved the men good-bye from the door-step, then hurried to make the beds and tidy the bedrooms before she left.

Emily was cleaning the kitchen and Neoma heard a sudden crash which meant that, as usual, she had smashed something.

For once she did not rush downstairs to see what it was. Instead, she went to her bedroom to change from the old dress she had worn to give Peregrine his breakfast into the gown in which she had returned from Syth yesterday.

"The Marquis will think I have only one gown to wear," she told herself, "and he will be right. But what does it matter? At least I will have my riding-habit with me this time."

Actually it was not her habit but her mother's, and it was therefore better-cut and of finer material than anything Neoma could have afforded since her parents' death.

There was a riding-hat to go with it, and though she put it in a hat-box and laid it on top of her trunk, she found herself remembering how the Marquis had said that he liked to see the sunshine on her hair.

'It was a funny thing for him to have said,' she thought.

He had said it in his cold, impersonal voice, which had made it a statement without any warmth in it.

"He is a strange man," Neoma told herself.

Driving beside him now, she thought the same thing, except that the word "strange" became "enigmatic."

She did not understand him, did not understand why his condition for saving Peregrine from having to pay the debt of honour involved her.

She was only thankful that she had been able to comply so easily.

She would have two nights and one whole day at Syth. By that time, she thought, the Marquis would very likely be relieved that she wished to leave early, so that without anyone being the wiser she could be back in London in plenty of time to cook Peregrine and Charles an exciting dinner.

She left Emily with the money to buy the meat she wanted and instructions to bring it into the house late on Saturday afternoon so that it would be fresh for Sunday.

She had also given her a list of other things she needed, for although Emily could not read, the tradesmen could do so.

'I hope I have remembered everything,' Neoma thought.

"I have a feeling," the Marquis said, "that you are worried. Why?"

"I am not really worried," Neoma replied. "I am enjoying feeling so important and up-in-the-world. This is the first time I have been in a Phaeton."

"You have never driven in one before?" the Marquis asked in astonishment.

Neoma laughed.

"The people I know have to walk, or if they are feeling rich they take a hackney-carriage."

As she spoke, she thought how much Peregrine would have enjoyed being able to drive a Phaeton of his own, and although she was sure he would never tool his horses as well as the Marquis, he would be infinitely better than some of the gentlemen they were passing on the road.

They were soon outside London and in the country, and Neoma looked round her with delight.

"How beautiful everything is," she said aloud. "I cannot imagine why anyone ever wants to live in a town."

"Think of all the parties you would miss," the Marquis said.

Neoma was just about to reply that she had never been to any parties in London, but she thought that in consequence he might think she was very dull.

'When he has been kind enough to invite me as his guest,' she thought to herself, 'I must try not to bore him.'

Because she knew it was one subject they had in common, she asked him about his horses and he told her how he had searched for a long time before he had found such a perfectly matched team.

Syth was looking even more awe-inspiring, Neoma thought, than when she had left it.

As they drove down the long drive and saw its dome above the trees she felt that she reached out towards it as if it were a familiar friend.

"It is lovely . . . lovely . . . lovely!" she said aloud.

Because there was a ring of unmistakable sincerity in her voice, the Marquis turned to look at her with a smile on his lips.

"I think," she said after a moment, "I quoted the wrong poet to you the other day, although you very likely have it marked in your book."

"I feel that there is a barb somewhere in what you are about to say," the Marquis said, "but let me hear it."

"Looking at Syth, it is obvious that you can say to yourself: *'I am Monarch of all I survey, My right there is none to dispute,'* " Neoma quoted.

The Marquis laughed.

"Again you have forgotten the end of the verse," he said:

" 'Better dwell in the midst of alarms, Than reign in this horrible place.' "

"That certainly does not apply!" Neoma cried. "No-one could say that Syth was not the most beautiful house in the whole world!"

Then as if she felt she had been too effusive, she added:

"But I suppose you will say I am not a very ... experienced judge."

"I should say nothing of the sort," the Marquis replied. "I like to hear my possessions admired, just as I am delighted to have compliments passed about myself."

Neoma looked at him in surprise.

"I always thought you were not interested in other people's opinions. Perhaps I was wrong."

"Shall I say it depends on the person who expresses them, and of course I am interested in what you think."

"About you?"

"Certainly!"

Neoma looked away from him towards the house.

"I was just thinking that you are enigmatic," she said, "but perhaps what I should really say is that you seem to me to contradict your 'reputation.' "

"What do you mean by that?" the Marquis enquired.

"They say you are ruthless but I know you can be kind," Neoma replied. "You appear to like disreputable people, but they are the opposite of yourself. And I am not certain ... but I think you ... understand what other people ... suffer, even though you would not ... admit it."

As she spoke, she thought the Marquis had understood about Peregrine, and she would always be inexpressibly grateful to him for not insisting that he must pay up.

She had only to remember Peregrine's gratitude and the way he had hugged her to feel inside herself a warmth for the Marquis because he had understood.

There was no time for him to reply to what she had said because they were crossing over the bridge and a few seconds later were turning in the courtyard to draw up outside the front door.

The red carpet was down and the usual array of footmen were waiting, and as Neoma was helped down from the Phaeton to join the Marquis on the steps, he said:

"Welcome to Syth!"

"It is exciting to be back!" Neoma answered.

As she walked into the Hall she looked at the Laguerre paintings on the walls, thinking how she had expected never to see them again once her visit to Syth was over.

They walked into the Salon and the Marquis insisted on Neoma having a little champagne before she went upstairs to get ready for luncheon.

Mrs. Elverton met her at the top of the stairs.

"It's nice to see you back, Miss," she said.

Although her words were affable, there was an expression on her face which Neoma thought was one of disapproval.

'I expect she is surprised that I have not brought a Chaperone with me,' she thought a little anxiously, 'and it would be impossible to explain to her why I could not do so.'

She expected to be shown into the bedroom where she had slept before, but they went farther along the corridor.

Because Neoma was worried about Mrs. Elverton she paid little attention to the room until she had taken off her bonnet and was tidying her hair.

Then it was the reflection in the mirror which made her realise how pretty the room was and she looked round her with delight.

There were brocade walls in turquoise blue and bed-hangings in the same colour under an enormous canopy carved with gilded cupids and doves.

It was as impressive as anything she had seen in the other rooms.

"Mr. Greystone did not show me this room," she said to herself, and thought with delight that when she had more time she would examine the pictures, which she could see were French and very attractive.

Now she knew that she must not keep the Marquis waiting, and, having washed her hands, she hurried down the stairs to join him, feeling that because there were no gaudily dressed women chattering in the Salon, or gentlemen like Lord Dadchett drinking, the whole place seemed more beautiful.

The Marquis was standing by the open window in the Salon looking out into the garden.

As Neoma joined him he asked:

"A little more champagne?"

"No, thank you."

She thought, as she spoke, how awful it would be if she ever drank too much or behaved as those women had done the first night she had arrived at Syth.

As if the Marquis knew what she was thinking, he said:

"Shall we forget what shocked and affronted you in my house and concentrate on enjoying it as it is, when there is no-one here but ourselves?"

"That is what I want to do," Neoma said with a smile, "and I feel that there is so much more for me to see, so much more to learn."

"And what will you do with such learning when you have acquired it?"

"Hold it in my memory," Neoma answered. "Then, if I am ever unhappy or worried, I can, with my imagination, stand in front of your pictures or walk round this room and know that everything I see, everything I touch, is a delight!"

She paused, then said:

"Perhaps that is the right way to learn history— to have a gallery of glorious memories that will in the future provide something to help and inspire us."

"And what about the failures and mistakes? There have been a great number of those in the past."

"Surely the lesson they teach us is never to make the same mistakes again."

"You are very optimistic," the Marquis remarked, "but that, after all, is the prerequisite of youth."

Luncheon was announced and they ate in the small Dining-Room, which was oval in shape and had pale apple-green walls. It was decorated not with pic-

tures but with statuary set in niches which revealed
the beauty of their classical proportions.

The Marquis had been to Greece and Neoma asked
him about the country she had always longed to see.

"I would like to show you the Acropolis," the
Marquis said, "especially under a full moon—then you
can live up to your name and be a part of its light."

"How wonderful that would be," Neoma said
wistfully.

"I am sure there must be a picture in this house
of the Acropolis. It has been painted by many famous
artists. You must ask Mr. Greystone."

"I am asking you," Neoma replied. "What you
own you should know."

"You are right," the Marquis agreed, "but I usually find that my guests are not interested in what I possess unless I am prepared to give it to them."

Neoma thought that that was because he asked
very strange types of persons to stay with him.

Because she did not wish to appear rude, she
went on talking about pictures until luncheon was
finished.

Then because they were to go riding she hurried
upstairs to change.

Mrs. Elverton had said as she showed her to her
bedroom:

"I expect you'd like Elsie to wait on you, Miss,
seeing as you know her already."

"I would like it very much," Neoma replied.

Now she found Elsie in her room, laying out her
riding-habit.

"You've brought your own habit this time, Miss,"
Elsie said. "Though I doubts if you'll need the jacket.
It's ever so hot today."

"Then I will just wear my blouse," Neoma said.

She felt that it was unconventional, but then the
Marquis preferred her not to wear a hat, which was
very unconventional too.

The skirt of her mother's habit fitted her perfectly
and made her waist look very small.

Just in case the Marquis might think she should be
properly attired, for it was not early in the morning as

it was when they had ridden before, she carried the jacket of her habit as she went down the stairs.

He was waiting for her in the Hall and he looked up as she started to descend. Because he was watching her she felt a little shy.

As she reached him she said in a low voice so that the footmen could not hear:

"I wondered if you would wish me to wear a jacket, although it is rather hot."

"You look exactly right as you are," the Marquis replied, and she thought his eyes rested on her hair.

She smiled at him and put her jacket down on a chair, then went down the steps to where the horses were waiting.

The Marquis lifted her into the saddle and when his hands were on her waist Neoma was acutely conscious of him in a way that she had never been before.

Then as they started to trot into the Park she forgot everything but the joy of riding a magnificent horse.

They rode for a longer distance than they had done in the mornings, and as they turned for home the Marquis said unexpectedly:

"Are you happy?"

"Of course I am!" Neoma answered. "How could I be anything but happy riding a horse like this?"

She leant forward as she spoke to pat her mount's neck.

"I see I shall have to give you a horse."

Neoma laughed, thinking that he was joking.

"It is a fascinating idea," she said, "but the inhabitants of Royal Avenue might be surprised to find him tied up at night to a lamp-post! Do you think we could squeeze him into the Dining-Room if we took away the table?"

She did not wait for the Marquis's reply but urged her horse into a trot, thinking, as she did so, that she must savour every second of the time she was at Syth because whatever else was in her gallery of memories, this would be the most important.

The afternoon passed quickly. There was tea in

one of the smaller Sitting-Rooms and afterwards they
went into the Library, where the Marquis showed Neoma precious first editions of authors and poets whom
she had read and loved for years.

"How have you managed to read so much in your
short life?" the Marquis asked.

"I read very quickly," Neoma confessed, "and I
also have a lot of time in which to read."

She thought he looked slightly sceptical, and she
very nearly told him of the long hours she had been
alone, first at the Manor after her parents' death, then
in London when Peregrine only came home to change
his clothes and otherwise she saw nobody but Emily.

She had brought a large number of books to London from the country, but she had also discovered a
Lending-Library and at first had gone back day after
day to change her books.

Then she had realised that although the fee was
very small she was being extravagant and she had ra-
tioned herself to three books a week or sometimes less
when she felt that the money must be spent on food
for Peregrine than rather selfishly on herself.

She looked round the Library and said:

"If you offered to give me any picture that I
fancied in the house or five hundred books from here,
I wonder which I would choose."

"I may be wrong," the Marquis said, "but I feel it
would be the books."

"You are right!" Neoma exclaimed. "At the same
time, it would be a very difficult decision to make when
I think of the Botticelli in the Silver Salon and the
Boucher in the French."

The Marquis raised his eye-brows.

"Did you know which those pictures were?" he
asked. "Or did Mr. Greystone tell you?"

"Naturally I have read about them and seen
sketches of them both," Neoma answered. "But Mr.
Greystone explained how they had come into the possession of your ancestors. He also knew a great deal
about the artists and their lives."

The Marquis glanced at the clock.

"It is nearly time for us to change for dinner,"

he said, "but before we go downstairs—as you were talking about presents, I have one to give to you."

"A present for me?"

Neoma's eyes lit up.

She had the feeling that it might be a book of poetry because they had quoted so many verses to each other, and she said as they walked towards the Salon:

"Shall I guess, or shall I shut my eyes until you give it to me?"

"Shut your eyes," the Marquis replied.

When they went into the Salon, Neoma put her hands over her eyes and said:

"I am waiting!"

She heard a drawer open and close. Then the Marquis came to her side.

"You may open your eyes now," he said.

She took away her hands and looked down to see that he was holding out to her a round leather box.

She was surprised because she had expected a book, but she took it from him and opened it.

For a moment she thought there must be some mistake, for the box contained a turquoise and diamond necklace lying on a bed of black velvet.

"I thought turquoises would become you," the Marquis said.

Neoma did not reply. She was merely very still, staring at the necklace, finding it difficult to understand that he in fact intended to give her such an expensive present.

As she had not spoken and in fact had not moved since she had opened the box, the Marquis asked:

"What is the matter? I thought it would please you."

There was a little pause before Neoma replied, not looking at him:

"I . . . do not want you to . . . think I am . . . ungrateful."

"But you do not like it! Why?"

"It is not that . . . of course I like it! It is very, very beautiful . . . but I cannot . . . accept it."

"Why not?"

The Marquis spoke sharply.

"Please . . . do not be . . . angry . . . it is very . . . very kind of you," Neoma murmured, "but . . . I could not . . . accept such a valuable present . . . from anyone!"

"Why not?" the Marquis asked again.

With a nervous little gesture Neoma shut the jewel-box.

"Please . . . try to understand," she begged, "but it would be . . . incorrect . . . somehow . . . wrong, because I have . . . nothing to give you in return."

She thought the Marquis was angry and added quickly:

"It is too . . . difficult to explain . . . but perhaps we can talk about it . . . later. I had better go and dress for dinner."

She walked away from him quickly, afraid to look at his face in case he was scowling, and when she reached the Hall she ran up the stairs to her bedroom.

Elsie was waiting for her and as she undressed and got into her bath Neoma could only wonder why the Marquis would want to buy her a present and one that she could not possibly accept.

Her mother would have been horrified at the idea of her accepting a present of any sort from a strange man!

She could only imagine that the Marquis was somehow trying to compensate for her being upset and shocked by the women who had been so drunk and behaved so badly the first night at dinner.

There was no other possible explanation for his gift, Neoma told herself.

Although she wanted to please him and show that she was grateful that he had even thought of her, she knew that she could not possibly take from him jewellery which must have cost hundreds of pounds.

Apart from anything else, how could she explain such a possession to Peregrine?

She worried over the necklace all the time she was dressing and Elsie was arranging her hair.

'I suppose,' Neoma thought at length, 'the Marquis is so rich that his buying a present like that is rather like another man purchasing a pair of gloves or a book.'

Whatever the explanation, she could not accept the necklace, and she only hoped it would not spoil their evening as it would if he was disagreeable.

However, when she reached the Salon she found that the Marquis was waiting for her and there was no scowl on his face and he was in fact smiling.

He offered her a glass of champagne and when she refused he did not press her.

"It will be the third dinner you have eaten at Syth," he said, "and I want you to enjoy yourself, and so you shall do exactly as you wish to do."

The fact that he was not angry gave Neoma a feeling of relief and something else warm and happy inside her.

It was a glow that seemed to deepen and intensify as the evening went by.

There was so much to talk about while they ate a most superlative dinner, and when the servants had withdrawn and there was only the light from the candles on the table, the Marquis sat back, a glass of brandy in his hand, and asked:

"Now, do you intend to quote Cowper, Donne, or Dryden?"

Dimples showed at each side of Neoma's mouth as she considered the question for a moment before she replied:

"You look undoubtedly god-like."

"Then I hope you will adhere to the final line of that particular verse."

Neoma thought for a moment, then she quoted:

" 'None but the brave deserves the fair.' "

"Exactly!" the Marquis said. "And without conceit I have always considered myself to be brave."

As he spoke, Neoma remembered the lines he had marked in the poem by John Donne: *No where lives a woman true and fair.*

She was certain that at some time in his life he had been disillusioned and obviously by a woman.

The Marquis was watching the expression in her

eyes. Then he put down his unfinished glass of brandy and said:

"Let us go into the Salon."

"You do not wish me to leave you to your port?"

"I do not want any port tonight," the Marquis replied, "and I have no wish for you to leave me."

They walked side-by-side down the corridor and into the Salon.

The curtains had been pulled and the candles lit.

One long French window, as if on the Marquis's instructions, was open onto the terrace outside.

Almost instinctively Neoma walked towards it.

They had sat so long over dinner that the sun had set, twilight had passed, and the stars had come out in the sky overhead.

The Marquis took her by the arm and they moved across the terrace to lean against the stone balustrade.

Down below them a mist was beginning to form round the trees in the Park.

The lake reflected the light from the sky and there was a crescent moon rising over the high trees.

Neoma looked up, her head thrown back.

"It is so beautiful!" she said in a low voice.

"And so are you, Light of the Moon," the Marquis answered.

She was so surprised at his words that she turned to look at him, and as she did so, his arms went round her and his lips were on hers.

For a moment she was too astonished to feel anything but incredulity that it could be happening.

She was too bemused, too bewildered to struggle, nor did she even think of freeing herself.

Then as the Marquis's arms tightened a little, she felt something strange happening within herself. The glow she had felt all the evening seemed to rise through her body and into her breasts and from them into her throat until it reached her lips.

She knew then that the pressure of the Marquis's mouth evoked a wonder that was different from anything she had known or thought possible.

It was as if all the beauty of Syth and the wonder of the sky above them was concentrated in the kiss that was the ecstasy she had always thought it would be and so much more.

It was everything that was beautiful and lovely, like music and paintings, and at the same time it was the happiness of riding and the holiness which was part of her prayers and of God Himself.

It flashed through her mind that this was love! This was love as she had dreamt of it and imagined it would be, only more wonderful, more perfect, and more sacred.

She felt the Marquis draw her closer still and she felt, although she did not understand it, the glow within her seeming to burn like a flame, and at the same time she felt as if she were no longer herself but a part of him.

Finally, when a century of time might have passed, the Marquis raised his head and Neoma felt as if the stars she could see round his head lit him with a light which came not only from the Heavens but from her own heart.

"I . . . love . . . you!"

She was not certain if she said the words aloud. She only knew they pulsated in every nerve of her body, in every corner of her mind.

This was love . . . love as she had always thought she would find it. How could she have guessed for one moment that it would be for the Marquis?

"That is what I want you to say, my sweet," the Marquis said, "and I have waited for what seemed to me a long time to hear you say it."

He looked down at her face for a long moment, then he said:

"But I need not wait any longer. Go upstairs and get into bed."

As he spoke he turned away from her to lean over the balustrade, as if he was preventing himself from stopping her from leaving him.

She looked at him a little uncertainly, and then because he had told her what to do she obeyed him, passing through the Salon and the Hall and up the stairs, barely aware of where she was going.

She could still feel his lips on hers and the feelings he had evoked in her moving through her body like music.

In a daze she walked along the corridor, thinking only that she must be in a dream—a dream that was so wonderful, so perfect, that she had touched the stars and it was hard to realise that she was back on earth again.

Just as she reached her room, a door opened a little farther down the passage and she saw a man whom she recognised as the Marquis's valet come through it, carrying a coat in his hand.

Because she knew she would find it difficult to say even "good-evening" at this moment, Neoma opened her own door.

The room was ablaze with lights. Then through another door, which she had not previously noticed, Elsie appeared.

"Oh, you're early, Miss!" she exclaimed. "I didn't expect you so soon."

Neoma could find no words to answer, and Elsie went on:

"I was just putting some more flowers, on His Lordship's instructions, in your *Boudoir*. Do look at them. Miss. They're really lovely!"

The maid opened the door farther, and because she could not think of any reason why she should refuse, Neoma followed her into a small room which was as exquisitely furnished as the bedroom.

The sofas and chairs were all covered in the same blue damask, and on the side-tables there were vases of flowers which filled the whole room with their fragrance.

"They're lovely, aren't they, Miss?" Elsie said, "and His Lordship's bedroom, as I expects you know, is over here."

She crossed the room as she spoke, opening a door on the other side.

Through the open door Neoma had a glimpse of a huge four-poster bed.

Just for a moment she stared at it automatically,

then suddenly, so suddenly that it was like a blow, she realised what Elsie had said.

"As I expects you know!"

Why would she know? Why should she think for one moment that she was in a bedroom next to the Marquis with a communicating-door as there had been to Peregrine's bedroom, except that in this instance there was a small Sitting-Room between them?

Then as if a veil were being wrenched away from Neoma's eyes she saw the women at dinner, the way the men were behaving with them, and she knew that each one had been paired with the other and their bedrooms had been adjoining as hers was now with the Marquis's!

Suddenly, like a harsh light compelling her to see and to understand, she knew why the Marquis had asked her to stay alone at Syth ... why he had offered her such a valuable present ... why after kissing her he had sent her upstairs to bed.

She gave an involuntary cry of sheer horror, and then running from the Sitting-Room and through her bedroom, she opened the door and ran down the passage.

There was only one place she wanted to go, one place she felt she would be safe, and that was the Chapel.

It seemed to her at that moment like a sanctuary in the midst of a holocaust so frightening, so terrifying, that instinctively she clung to the only thing she knew could save her.

She ran down the long corridors past Mr. Greystone's office, then at last, breathless, she reached the Chapel.

The door stood open, and just as the rest of the house was lit so there were two six-branched candelabra alight on the altar.

Neoma threw herself down on her knees, and although she wanted to pray no words would come.

Instead she could only see as if it were emblazoned indelibly on her mind the degredation of the women at the Dining-Room table, the glinting emerald necklace round Vicky Vale's neck, and the look in Lord Dadchett's eyes as he tried to kiss her.

It was all part of what she had not understood but it now rose up like a monster to terrify her with its implications.

The way the women talked, the familiarity with which the gentlemen treated them, and the things Peregrine had said that she had not understood were all there.

At last the words she wanted to say came to her lips:

"Help me, God! Help me! How could I have been so ... foolish as to have ... come here? How ... could I not have ... understood?"

Then because she was frightened she cried out for her mother and the tears came into her eyes and ran down her cheeks.

"I am sorry, Mama ... I am sorry that I have been so ... stupid ... but I did not ... understand ... I did not realise there were things ... like this in the world."

She murmured the words beneath her breath and as they were choked by sobs she heard a step behind her, and she stiffened.

For a moment it was impossible to move. Then she knew that the Marquis was there and somehow she had to explain to him, had to make him understand.

She turned her head as if to assure herself that it was he, then slowly she got to her feet and walked towards him.

There was a look of surprise and puzzlement on his face as he saw her frightened eyes and the tears on her cheeks.

"What is it?" he asked. "What has upset you?"

Neoma clasped her hands together and in a voice that did not sound like her own she said:

"I ... I did not ... know ... I had no idea ... please believe me ... I did not understand what you ... meant when you ... asked me to ... stay ... or why you had asked me."

"What did you not understand?"

"What . . . those women did . . . or why they had
rooms next to the gentlemen they came with . . . I
thought it was just because they were . . . f-friends . . .
but I know now . . . why Peregrine said he could not
pay anybody . . . to come with him. It . . . seemed
strange . . . but I thought it was because they were . . .
losing their . . . earnings at the Theatres."

The Marquis, with his eyes on Neoma's face,
seemed stunned into silence.

Then after a moment she went on, still in a
frightened, lost little voice:

"I . . . know how . . . ignorant I must seem to you
. . . but I never knew . . . women were . . . like that . . .
or that men like . . . y-you would think them . . . attractive. It was foolish . . . so very foolish. Please . . .
forgive me . . . but I cannot . . . d-do what you want,
because it would be . . . wrong and w-wicked."

"Wrong and wicked?" the Marquis repeated. "Are
you telling me that Standish is not your lover?"

"N-no, of course not . . . how can you think . . ."
Neoma began indignantly.

She was just about to say that Peregrine was her
brother, when she realised that it would do him
harm.

Of course the Marquis would be shocked at the
idea of his bringing his sister to a party where the
women behaved in such a degrading manner and the
men paid them to do so.

"Are you telling me the truth?" the Marquis de-
manded.

Neoma raised her face to his as if she was surprised at the question. Then when she saw the expression in his eyes she said:

"I should . . . never have . . . come here with
P-Peregrine. I know that . . . now. In fact I knew it
the first . . . night that we arrived . . . but I wanted to
h-help him."

"Of course!" the Marquis said. "He relied on your
help to steal the IOU."

Neoma was still for a moment, then she asked:

"If I do not . . . do what you . . . want . . . will
you make Peregrine . . . pay?"

Her voice trembled and her eyes filled with tears again as she spoke.

The Marquis looked at her, then he said very quietly:

"Suppose we talk about this tomorrow? I think you are tired and I think too you have had an unexpected shock."

As she spoke he took his handkerchief from his pocket and wiped Neoma's eyes.

Because he was so gentle she felt even more as if she wanted to cry.

"Go to bed, Neoma," the Marquis said. "Lock your door and I promise you will not be disturbed by me or anybody else."

She looked up at him, her wet eye-lashes dark against the fairness of her skin.

"You are . . . not angry with . . . me?"

"No, of course not," the Marquis replied. "Only bewildered, because like you I have been extremely stupid."

She looked puzzled and he said:

"Stop worrying about it tonight. There is tomorrow, and the horses will be waiting for us."

Neoma tried to smile, but the tears were still in her eyes.

"I have been so . . . very . . . very foolish."

"I think the answer is that you are very, very young."

"Why did nobody . . . tell me of such . . . things?"

Her voice broke on the words.

"We agreed you would forget about it until tomorrow," the Marquis said. "Come along. I am going to take you to the bottom of the stairs, and I think you can find your own way from there."

As he spoke he slipped his arm through hers and drew her along the corridor and back to the Hall.

At the foot of the stairs he took her hand and raised it to his lips.

"Good-night, Neoma. Sleep well," he said. "Shall we ride before breakfast, or would you rather wait until afterwards?"

"I . . . I would like to ride early."

"Then shall we say half-past-seven?"

"I will be . . . ready."

She looked for a moment at the Marquis's eyes, and felt something flicker within her as she had felt when he had kissed her.

Then because she was afraid of her own feelings she hurried up the stairs, not looking back, and finding it hard to breathe until she reached her own bedroom.

Chapter Seven

Riding back to Syth across the Park, Neoma looked at the Marquis for almost the first time.

When she had come downstairs to ride with him she had felt too shy, and she was also afraid that she would see on his face that look of contempt and disdain that always made her feel insignificant.

When she had got into bed the night before she could not help crying tempestuously. Then she had found herself thinking of the kiss the Marquis had given her and the inexpressible rapture his lips had aroused in her.

For a moment her tears and her unhappiness were forgotten and all she could think of was the wonder of his arms and the way in which he had seemed to carry her up to the stars.

Then she told herself dismally that she had felt that way only because she was ignorant and inexperienced.

To the Marquis she was just another Vicky Vale or any of the other "high-steppers," as Peregrine had called them, whom he had kissed.

But she knew that she would never be able to forget the ecstasy he had aroused in her and which she knew summed up everything she had ever thought love should be.

She slept but fitfully, having unhappy dreams in which she was running down long corridors and could find nowhere to hide.

Yet when Elsie knocked on her door in the morning and she let her in, she felt an irrepressible excitement because she could ride again with the Marquis.

Nevertheless, it was difficult to go downstairs and face him.

His voice was quiet as he wished her good-morning. Then as she moved ahead of him out into the sunshine, she felt, as he lifted her into the saddle, that the colour rose in her cheeks.

He did not say anything. He merely adjusted her skirt over the stirrup, then mounted his own horse and they rode off as they had before, moving under the shade of the trees until they came to a flat piece of grassland on which they could gallop.

'He may be angry with me, he may send me back to London today,' Neoma thought, 'but at least I shall have had the joy of this last ride.'

At the back of her mind was still the fear that despite what he had said, the Marquis might make Peregrine pay the two thousand pounds because she would not fulfil her part of the bargain.

'How could I ever have . . . guessed that was what he . . . meant?' she wondered despairingly.

Then insidiously a thought came to her mind: perhaps if the Marquis made love to her, it would be as wonderful as his kiss had been!

She was shocked at herself for thinking such a thing, and yet the thought persisted and made her feel shyer than ever.

Only when they turned back and Syth lay in front of them, very lovely as the morning sunshine glistened on the hundreds of windows, turning them to gold, did the Marquis say:

"Would you like to ride again this afternoon?"

Neoma felt her heart leap.

At least he did not wish her to leave at once! She wanted to stay, wanted to talk to him, even though she was afraid of what he might say.

"It would be . . . wonderful!" she answered. "If that is what you . . . want to do too."

"There is a lake on the southern part of the estate which you have not seen," he replied. "Sometimes there are rare birds nesting on it, such as Canadian geese."

"I would love to see them," Neoma replied.

They rode on and when they reached the house the Marquis said:

"It is later than we usually are, so I suggest we have breakfast immediately, before you change. I must admit to feeling quite hungry."

Neoma was not hungry because she still felt the constriction inside her which had been there since last night when she had run to the Chapel for sanctuary.

It was not as tight in her breasts as it had been, but she knew she would find it difficult to eat, although she did not tell the Marquis so.

She pulled off her riding-jacket, which she had worn because it was quite cool early in the morning, and put it down on a chair at the bottom of the stairs, then followed the Marquis into the Breakfast-Room.

There was the usual array of silver dishes, all containing enough food, Neoma thought, for a dozen people.

"What can I get you?" the Marquis asked.

As she thought it would annoy him if she said that she wished nothing, she let him help her to scrambled eggs with mushrooms as she sat down at the table and sipped the fragrant coffee, hoping that in some magical way it would disperse her shyness.

She was acutely conscious of the Marquis as he sat opposite her, and she wondered if last night he had thought of their kiss, and if after all she had said, he would ever want to kiss her again.

Perhaps she had been wrong to let him do so in the first place, but it had not seemed wrong at the time. It had seemed right, wonderful, and perfect, and whatever happened afterwards it was a part of God.

"You are not eating," the Marquis commented, breaking in on her thoughts. "There are a lot of things I want to show you today, and I cannot have you fainting on my hands for want of food!"

Neoma knew that he was teasing her, but she answered quite seriously:

"I will not do that."

"First of all," the Marquis said, "we must go to the stables. I fear that my horses which you have not yet seen are feeling neglected."

Neoma was just going to say that it was something she wanted to do more than anything else, when suddenly the door of the Dining-Room was flung open and Peregrine walked into the room.

She was so astonished to see him that for a moment she could only stare, before she exclaimed:

"Peregrine! What are you . . . doing here?"

Peregrine, however, was looking at the Marquis, and there was an expression on his face that Neoma had never seen before.

"I ought to kill you!" he cried harshly, and his voice seemed to echo round the room.

Neoma rose to her feet.

"What are you . . . saying? What is the . . . matter?"

"You ask me what is the matter," Peregrine answered in a furious voice, "when I find you here alone with this devil?"

Neoma tried to speak but her voice seemed to stick in her throat, and Peregrine went on:

"What do you think I felt when Dadchett told me he had seen you driving out of London towards Syth and asked me what this reprobate had paid for you!"

He drew in his breath sharply before he added:

"He even said that whatever I had received, he would double it!"

"Peregrine!"

It was a cry of horror.

"I daresay it is all my fault," he said, still in a furious voice, "for bringing you to this sink of iniquity in the first place, but I hardly expected to have my sister bid for as if she were a common prostitute!"

He glared at the Marquis, who had not moved since he had come into the room, and went on as if he could not check the words pouring from his lips:

"I am not entirely brainless, and when Dadchett said that, I knew exactly what had happened. You have forced Neoma to pay your price for an IOU which is not worth the paper it was written on."

He almost spat the words as he spoke. Then he said:

"I suppose if I were man enough I would challenge you to a duel, but if you killed me, doubtless you would get my sister cheaper than you have got her already! I am taking her away and tomorrow I will leave the deed of my estate at your house in London."

Neoma gave a little cry, but he paid no heed and merely finished:

"I doubt if it is worth the money I owe you, but I have nothing else of any value to give you, so you must make the best of it!"

He spoke rudely, his voice still fierce with anger.

Then he put out his hand towards Neoma, who had moved to his side while he was talking, and seized her by the arm.

"Come along," he said. "I am not allowing you to stay under this roof one moment longer."

"Peregrine!" Neoma protested.

"You are leaving now!" Peregrine said.

There was such a note of authority in his voice that she felt as if he was completely changed from the brother she had always looked after and mothered.

Without saying any more, Peregrine strode from the room, dragging Neoma with him.

She wanted to look back, to speak to the Marquis, to say once again that she was sorry, but Peregrine was moving too fast, and as they reached the Hall she knew despairingly that the Marquis had not followed them.

Breathless at the speed at which they had moved, she managed to gasp before they reached the door:

"My . . . trunk . . . my things are not . . . packed."

Peregrine stopped by the Major Domo.

"Kindly have Miss Standish's trunk taken to His Lordship's house in London tomorrow morning," he said, "and I will arrange to collect it."

"Very good, Sir."

While Peregrine was speaking, Neoma managed

to snatch her riding-jacket from the chair. Then, still holding her by the arm, he pulled her down the steps and she saw that there was a chaise outside, drawn by two horses.

There was a groom at their heads, and as Peregrine took the reins, he jumped up into the seat behind them.

They drove off and had reached the end of the drive before Neoma realised what had happened and found her voice.

"I am . . . sorry."

"We will talk about it when we get home," Peregrine said. "If he has hurt you, I swear I will kill him!"

"No, no! I am . . . all right. It is . . . not what you . . . think," Neoma managed to say.

She spoke barely above a whisper, conscious that the groom sitting behind might be able to hear her.

She thought that the anger on Peregrine's face lightened a little, but he did not speak and they drove for a long while in silence.

Only as Neoma realised that they had turned off the main London road did she ask:

"Where are we . . . going?"

"To the Manor," Peregrine replied. "I have to collect the deed, as you are well aware."

She felt the tears gather in her eyes.

It was not only at the thought that her home would be lost forever, but that once it had gone, Peregrine would have nothing left. However, she thought despairingly that there was no point in saying so.

She knew that he would do as he had said and hand over the deed to the Marquis in payment of his "debt of honour."

"O God," she asked in her heart, "how could You have let this happen? Why did Peregrine have to find out?"

*   *   *

It was a long journey across country and it was late in the afternoon before they turned down the familiar drive with its empty, dilapidated lodges and rusting iron gates.

Perhaps it was in contrast to Syth that Neoma found herself noticing that broken branches of trees were lying on the uncut grass and everything round the ancient house was overgrown to the point of wildness.

The Elizabethan bricks, however were, still the warm, weather-beaten pink which had survived for more than two centuries.

Although the glass was broken in the upstairs windows and there were a number of tiles missing off the roof, Neoma knew that she loved it and that it was a part of her blood just as it was Peregrine's inheritance.

'And now we have lost it,' she thought. 'Lost it to a man to whom it can mean nothing when he has so much.'

And yet somehow in the back of her mind she thought that the Marquis would understand that she loved it because it was beautiful and because it was where she belonged.

"I must not think about him," she told herself.

As she walked into the house, knowing that as the old Briggses were deaf they would not hear her arrival, she knew that Peregrine was tipping the groom, although it was something he could not afford to do.

She went into the Sitting-Room. The curtains and covers were old and faded and the carpet was almost threadbare, but it was warm and familiar with memories of her mother.

Neoma longed, as she had never longed before, for her to be there, ready to listen to their troubles and solve them in her own inimitable fashion.

However, it was not her mother but Peregrine who came through the doorway, and she knew that he was still angry.

"How could you have done anything so reprehensible as to listen to the Marquis?" he asked.

"Must we ... talk about it?" Neoma asked in a small voice.

She felt that she could not bear to explain to

Peregrine how she had not understood what was expected of her or tell him how the Marquis had offered her a valuable necklace.

"You say he has not touched you?" Peregrine asked fiercely.

Neoma shook her head.

Again she could not tell Peregrine that the Marquis had kissed her, and she knew, although she was very ignorant on the matter, that he was asking her if something more than a kiss had taken place between them.

"I am going upstairs to change," she said quickly, thinking that Peregrine might have other questions to ask. "Then I will find out what there is for dinner."

Peregrine did not reply, and as she was leaving the room she saw him fling himself down sulkily in one of the arm-chairs.

She felt he was thinking that he was missing a good dinner at Sir Edmund's house, just as he had missed the Mill, to come to rescue her.

He must have left at dawn, she thought, and she imagined after what he had learnt from Lord Dadchett he would have lain awake all night worrying about her and at the same time being violently incensed with the Marquis.

'It would be Lord Dadchett who had to upset everything!' she thought bitterly.

Because she had not told Peregrine that he had tried to kiss her, she knew that the knowledge that he had offered to buy her must have been more of a shock than it would otherwise have been.

'Everything I have . . . done seems to have been . . . wrong,' she thought hopelessly.

Then she wished, as so many others have done, that she could undo the past.

*   *   *   *

Neoma arranged the roses she had picked from the garden on the ancient Refectory-table in the Hall and found the tears gathering in her eyes as she did so.

Ever since Peregrine had left first thing in the

morning, with the deed to the Manor in his pocket, Neoma had found herself saying good-bye to everything she had known and loved since she was a child.

Peregrine had said very little, but she knew that it hurt him too and there was a white look round his mouth that she had not seen since her mother had died.

"When I come back this evening," he had said, "I will bring a carriage of some sort in which you can take away what you want to keep."

"Will the Marquis not give us . . . time to . . . move?" Neoma had asked in a low voice.

"What do we want time for?" Peregrine asked roughly. "If we have to go, considering how little the place is worth, we can hardly be dishonest and remove anything which will appreciate in price."

Neoma had given a little cry.

"I must keep some of Mama's special treasures— you know I . . . cannot part with . . . those!"

Peregrine shrugged his shoulders.

"I do not suppose they will matter to the Marquis one way or the other," he said. "At the same time, I wish to be under no obligation to him."

It was very touching, Neoma thought, that he should mind about her or sacrifice so much on her behalf.

At the same time, she knew that while Peregrine was loathing the Marquis with a bitterness that was understandable, she could only think of him in a very different way.

Last night when she had pleaded with him, he had wiped her eyes and sent her to bed alone.

She could not help feeling that in the same circumstances, anyone like Lord Dadchett would have behaved very differently.

But what was the point of trying to explain this to Peregrine when he was so angry?

Then he had gone, riding a horse that he had borrowed from a local farmer, which was very unlike anything that was stabled at Syth.

The two old horses in their own stables would have found the journey to London too far.

Neoma went to pat them and make a fuss of them,

thinking that when they became the property of the Marquis he would doubtless have them killed because they were of no use to him or to anyone else.

When she went back to the house she started to collect together the things that had been her mother's, as Peregrine had advised her to do.

After taking several armfuls to the Hall, she suddenly asked herself what was the use of it.

If the house in Royal Avenue should be sold over their heads, they would have to find somewhere else to live and a large amount of possessions would prove not only inconvenient but also expensive.

As she thought of Royal Avenue tears ran down her cheeks simply because it came to her mind more forcefully than ever before that with the Manor gone there would be nothing to look forward to in the future.

All the time she had been in London she had always been dreaming of the moment when they would go back home and she would look out onto the gardens and the fields beyond.

She would breathe in air, fragrant and fresh with flowers, and there would be the old Briggses to talk to about her father and mother instead of the hopeless task of making Emily understand what she wanted.

She went up to the bedroom which had always been her mother's. Then as if she could no longer control her emotions she flung herself down on the bed to cry until she could cry no more.

As she did so, she knew that she was crying not only for the loss of the Manor but also because she had lost the Marquis.

"I love him! Mama . . . I love . . . him!" she cried despairingly.

She knew that the future would always be empty because he was not there.

She knew too, just as if someone had told her so, that never again with any other man would she feel the rapture and wonder that he had given her when he had kissed her beneath the stars with the crescent moon rising up the sky.

Peregrine might think he was wicked and debauched, he might be ruthless and cruel to other people, but she kept remembering the gentleness of his hands as he wiped her tears and the kindness in his voice when he had said good-night.

"Why...why do I have to love...someone who is as...far away from me as the...moon in the sky?"

She remembered how he had called her Light of the Moon, and there had been a note in his voice that had not been there before.

The memory made her cry again, and finally when she was exhausted she lay for a long time on her mother's bed, listening to the birds singing outside the open window, knowing that she would never hear them again once she had left for London.

Finally, because she was ashamed of herself for having lost control and let her unhappiness overwhelm her, Neoma got up and washed her face in cold water and went down the stairs to arrange Peregrine's dinner.

There was very little in the house, but old Briggs said he would walk to the village and Neoma gave him the last few shillings she possessed to buy what was required.

At luncheon-time she had eaten a little bread and cheese, but there was nothing else in the house, and she knew that Peregrine, however desperate the straits they were in or the darkness of the future ahead, would still be hungry and want a good meal.

"I must try to be happy for the last hours we are here," Neoma told herself.

Because the house looked bare without flowers, she went into the garden to pick some roses.

The rose-garden which her mother had loved had been her special pride. It was now overgrown with weeds, but the roses, pink, white, and yellow, were just beginning to come into flower and their fragrance and the softness of their petals seemed to ease a little of the agony in her heart.

But it was difficult to think of anything but the Marquis and she kept wondering what he had done when they left.

Had he been angry at Peregrine's rudeness and

told himself that in the circumstances he was well rid of her?

Perhaps he had gone back to London to Vicky Vale, and she felt her whole being cry out at the thought.

"I love ... him!" she admitted. "But ... what is the use? I have to ... try to forget him."

She pushed a rose hard into the vase as if to relieve her feelings, and as she did so, a thorn ran into her finger.

It was only a slight prick, but the physical pain seemed to intensify the pain in her heart and the ache in her breast.

Tears ran down her cheeks again and as they did so, she heard someone come in through the open front door.

"Peregrine is back already!" she told herself. "He must not find me crying."

She tried to wipe away the tears with the back of her hand, then as she turned round to tell Peregrine that he was back quicker than she had expected, she saw that it was not her brother facing her but the Marquis!

For a moment she thought she must be imagining him and had conjured him up out of her very unhappiness.

Then there was no mistaking that, handsome and elegant, the Marquis was actually there. He put his hat and riding-gloves down on the end of the table where she was arranging the flowers and came a little nearer to her.

He did not speak and after a moment Neoma said nervously:

"Why ... are you ... here? Peregrine has ... gone to London to ... see you."

"I have seen him," the Marquis said, "but I wanted to talk to you."

She looked at him wide-eyed, finding it hard to take in what he was saying, and after a moment he said gently:

"As I have quite a lot to say, it would be more comfortable if we sat down."

"Yes . . . yes . . . of course," Neoma said. "Will you . . . come into the . . . Sitting-Room?"

She put the roses she was holding down beside the vase and led the way through the door behind her.

The sunshine was coming through the diamond-paned window and it turned Neoma's hair to gold as she stood in the centre of the room, looking at the Marquis.

She was afraid that he might look angry, but instead she saw that his expression was merely serious. Then he exclaimed:

"Your finger is bleeding!"

She looked down to see that the thorn had drawn blood, not much, but it was a crimson patch on her white skin.

The Marquis drew his handkerchief from his breast-pocket and, taking her hand in his, wiped away the blood.

She felt herself quiver because his fingers were touching hers.

He must have known what she felt, for he looked at her, and as their eyes met, it seemed to Neoma that not only did he understand what she was feeling but that it was impossible for her to look away.

For what seemed a long moment they were both very still. Then the Marquis said:

"Sit down, Neoma, I want to talk to you."

She obeyed him, sitting in the chair by the empty fireplace where her mother had always sat.

The Marquis stood for a moment looking down at her, then he sat down opposite.

"I have a lot of explaining to do," he said, "and as that is something I have never done before, it is difficult to know quite where to begin."

Neoma looked at him in surprise and he added:

"Somehow I think you will understand, but I am not sure."

"I will . . . try to understand . . . anything you have to tell me."

She was still feeling that tremor which had run through her when the Marquis had touched her hand.

It flashed through her mind that if he was going to leave her, perhaps he would kiss her just once again before he went out of her life forever.

The Marquis looked away from her towards the sunlit window, then he said:

"I was just two weeks from my twenty-first birthday when my father told me he had arranged my marriage."

"Y-your . . . marriage?" Neoma exclaimed.

She had never thought of him as being married and Peregrine had never suggested that he might be.

"Ever since I was a child," the Marquis said, "it had been drummed into me how important my position in life was and how when the time came, I must have a son to carry on the name and inherit Syth."

Neoma was listening intently, her hands clasped together in her lap, her eyes on the Marquis's face.

"My father told me that he had discussed my marriage with the Duke of Hull, who had a daughter a year older than I was. I tried to expostulate that I wanted a great deal more time as a bachelor before I was finally tied down in matrimony, but my father did not listen."

Neoma remembered that she had seen a picture of the fifth Earl at Syth and thought he looked very autocratic and overpowering.

"I was invited to stay with the Hulls at their Castle in Northumberland," the Marquis went on, "and when I saw the girl I was expected to marry, I was swept off my feet at her appearance."

"She was so . . . beautiful?"

"Very beautiful!" the Marquis replied. "Lucille was, in fact, every man's dream of what the woman he would marry should look like."

Neoma felt a stab of jealousy she had never known before.

'It is what I might have expected,' she thought, 'that the Marquis would find a beautiful wife who would be the counterpart of his own good looks.'

"I was very young and very idealistic," the Marquis continued, and now there was a sarcastic note in his voice that had not been there before. "I suppose you could say that I worshipped Lucille from the moment I saw her."

Neoma drew in her breath.

It was difficult to listen to him saying such things without feeling hurt and agonised by it.

"I wrote her poems which were as passionate and romantic as anything composed by John Donne," the Marquis continued, "and she told me she loved me."

There was a pause before he said:

"I was eager to be married and my father and the Duke saw no reason why we should wait. To me it was as if the gates of Heaven had been opened especially for me."

Neoma made a little movement with her hands, but she did not speak and the Marquis continued:

"We were married in Northumberland and came south to Syth, staying at various houses loaned to us by friends."

The Marquis glanced at Neoma for a moment, then away again before he said:

"I do not have to tell you that as the war was on we could not go abroad as I would have wished to do. I wanted to take Lucille for our honeymoon to Venice and I promised her that that was what I would do as soon as Napoleon was defeated."

Neoma thought that to be in Venice with the Marquis would certainly be Paradise for her and she wondered why it hurt her so much to hear him saying these things.

It was in fact agony to listen to him speaking of what he had felt for another woman.

"We stopped in London on the way to Syth," the Marquis was saying, "and Lucille persuaded me to buy her a great deal of jewellery, which I was only too willing to do. In fact there was an endless amount of things that she needed, but when one loves somebody one is always eager to give them presents."

As he spoke, Neoma thought of the turquoise and diamond necklace he had offered her. Then she told herself despairingly that it had not been given in love, but for a very different reason.

"Finally we arrived at Syth," the Marquis continued, "and although Lucille had stayed there once before we were married, there were so many things I wanted to show her, so many things I felt we could do together."

Neoma found the tears gathering in her eyes.

The Marquis and the woman he loved would have ridden together, she thought, as she had ridden on his superb horses in the early-morning sunshine.

There was a pause before the Marquis said in a hard voice:

"Two days after we arrived, Lucille ran away!"

He rose to his feet as he spoke, almost as if that made it easier to speak of it than when he was sitting down.

"Ran ... away?" Neoma questioned.

"She left me a note," the Marquis said, "telling me she was going to the man she loved, and as he had little money and I had plenty, she was taking what she thought she had earned by listening to my drooling sentiments when her heart was elsewhere!"

"Oh ... no!"

"She took with her everything I had given her and a great deal more besides," the Marquis went on, "some of the family jewels, miniatures which hung in the Salons, and snuff-boxes ornamented with diamonds and therefore very valuable."

"How cruel! How horrible!"

"I could not believe it had really happened. Then my father arrived to stay, and when he learnt what had occurred, he ordered me to follow Lucille to Ireland and bring her back."

His lips tightened before he continued:

"I realised then that he knew far more about the position than I did. In fact it was my father who told me that Lucille was in love with a penniless Irish Peer, a distant cousin of the Duke, who had been turned out of the Castle when he had wanted to marry her."

"Your father knew she was in love with ... another man when he ... arranged your marriage?"

"Yes, and the Duke knew it too," the Marquis said grimly, "for he was the one who had told my father the position, and yet they still thought the marriage a suitable one!"

"That was cruel! Wicked!"

"It was also humiliating. I told my father I had no intention of following my wife, nor did I wish ever to see her again."

"What did he say?"

"He went to Ireland himself and fought the duel he had ordered me to fight, wounding the Peer almost fatally!"

Neoma gasped and the Marquis went on:

"He then brought Lucille back with him by sheer force to Syth and ordered us both to live together as man and wife and make the best of the situation."

There was silence for a moment, then Neoma asked:

"What . . . did you . . . do?"

"I did nothing," the Marquis answered. "Lucille escaped at the first opportunity, only this time she did not even bother to leave me a note telling me of her intention."

Again there was a pause before he went on:

"She was drowned crossing the Irish Sea in a storm. Because she was in such a hurry to reach her lover, she had hired an unsound fishing-vessel which capsized!"

"How . . . did you . . . feel?"

"It is difficult to describe my feelings at that time," the Marquis answered. "Bitterness and an abject humiliation, besides a hatred of everyone concerned in the farcical situation. Also, because of my father's anger at what had occurred and the effort he had made in bringing Lucille back from Ireland, he had a heart-attack. In fact, he died within the year."

The Marquis stared with unseeing eyes out the window in front of him, and after what seemed a long time he said:

"What happened made me not only hate the woman who had been my wife and whom I had loved with the passionate intensity of the very young, but it also made me hate my father and everything for which he stood."

Again the Marquis's tone was bitter as he said:

"I considered him and the Duke to be upholders of what I felt was a dying tradition—that blue blood must be mixed with blue blood and nothing mattered except the continuation of the family."

"I can ... understand why you ... felt like ... that."

"I have told you this," the Marquis said, "because I wanted you to hear my answer to your question as to why I have behaved as I have for many years."

His voice was harsh as he continued:

"I joined the Army and went to Portugal under Wellington's command. Every time I killed a Frenchman, I thought I was killing part of the false ideals that had humiliated me in my marriage."

Neoma looked up at him and thought she was beginning to understand.

"When the war was over," the Marquis went on, "every time some drunken fool lost money to me or degraded himself in my house or at my dinner-table, I felt I was paying the whole of society back for what I had suffered and the manner in which I had been deceived and exploited."

Now Neoma knew why she had thought that, sitting at the top of the table watching the vulgarity and debauchery of his guests, he seemed like a male Circe, turning those he entertained into swine.

"I also swore to myself," the Marquis said, "that never again would I fall in love. Never again would I trust any woman."

His lips twisted in a mocking smile as he said:

"I chose to associate only with women who openly and honestly sold their favours for money. With them I knew exactly where I was, and there was no question of my ever being hurt."

Neoma had a vision of Vicky Vale's attractive, spectacular appearance, her slanting eyes, her provocative red mouth, and the manner in which she deliberately enticed the Marquis.

She felt she could bear no more. She could not

listen to him talking of such women when she loved
him.

Then she remembered how much he had suffered,
and suddenly he seemed to her like Peregrine—young
and vulnerable—who had got into trouble through no
fault of his own and did not know how to get out of
it.

She felt as if she must protect and look after the
Marquis even as she wanted to protect and look after
Peregrine.

"I am . . . sorry," she said in a soft voice, "so very
. . . very sorry for you."

"I do not want your commiseration," the Marquis replied. "I just want you to understand why I am
as I am."

"I do understand now, but it all happened a long
. . . time ago. You cannot go on . . . hating everybody
for . . . ever."

"That is what I have only just found out," the
Marquis said. "I thought my hatred was so much a
part of myself that nothing would ever change it. Then
I met you!"

He said the last words softly and Neoma thought
that she could not have heard him aright. As she
looked up at him in a startled fashion he went on:

"I have come here to ask you one very simple
question, and I want you to answer me truthfully."

"What . . . is it?"

"Yesterday when I kissed you," the Marquis
said, "you told me that you loved me. I want to know if
that is true—really true."

Neoma drew in her breath.

Somehow she could not speak, could not answer,
and the Marquis said:

"I know you pray. That means you believe in
God. As if you were standing before God, I want you
to answer that question with the truth—the whole
truth. I could not bear to be lied to again."

Almost as if he had told her to do so, Neoma
rose to her feet.

Her eyes seemed to fill her whole face, and in a
voice that was so low he could hardly hear it she said:

"When you . . . kissed me . . . it was the most . . . wonderful thing that had . . . ever happened . . . and I knew that I . . . loved you. When I left you . . . yesterday and thought that I would never . . . see you again . . . I knew it would be . . . impossible for me ever to . . . love anybody else in my . . . life."

Her voice died away to silence, but the Marquis did not move. He only stood looking at her, searching her face as if he would look deep into her soul.

Then he said:

"Are you sure? Are you quite sure that despite the way I have behaved, despite what I suggested to you . . ."

"That was not your fault," Neoma said quickly. "It was because when I came to Syth with Peregrine we lied in not telling you I was his sister, because Charles said people would be shocked. He said Peregrine would be ostracised if it was known he had taken me to one of your . . . notorious parties."

"It is something that should never have happened," the Marquis said, "and will never happen again."

There was a faint smile on his lips as he added:

"I am asking you to marry me, my darling. God knows I am not good enough for you in any way, but if you love me, perhaps you can overlook all my sins and just remember that I love you too!"

He saw the sudden light come into Neoma's eyes and there was a radiance in her face as if there were a light beneath her skin.

Then she said in a whisper:

"You . . . do . . . really love me?"

"I love you as I have never loved anyone in my life," the Marquis answered, "and that is the truth! What I felt long ago was the romantic emotion of an unfledged youth. What I feel now is very different. But I am afraid—desperately afraid!"

"Afraid!"

"That I may have spoilt something so perfect, so pure and lovely, that like fairy-gold it has vanished at the touch of human hands."

His voice deepened as he asked:

"Have I spoilt what you felt for me, my precious?"

He did not move, but Neoma moved a little nearer to him.

"If we have . . . lost it, I would feel as if the . . . sun would never . . . shine again . . . and I would always be in . . . darkness."

She paused, then added:

"I am . . . sure that if you . . . kiss me . . . we will . . . find that it is . . . still there."

She only whispered the words, but the Marquis heard them.

He put his arms out, she moved into them, and he held her very gently against him.

"Oh, my little Light of the Moon," he said. "I am frightened! Terribly frightened! Having found you, I think it would kill me if I lost you!"

"That is . . . how I felt . . . when I . . . thought I had . . . lost you."

The Marquis drew her closer, and slowly, as if he was half-afraid but at the same time savouring the moment, his lips found hers.

Just for one agonising flash of time Neoma thought that the wonder she had felt before had gone. Then like a streak of lightning running through her it was there—moving up through her body, and from her throat into her lips.

The room swung round her and everything that was beautiful that she had felt before passed between them, but more insistently, more poignantly, because they had both suffered.

She thought she had lost him, but he was there, holding her captive with his lips, his arms giving her a sense of security that she had never expected to feel again.

"I love . . . you! I love . . . you!" she tried to say.

It was a paean of joy that flew up into the sky above their heads, finding not the stars but the very heart of the sun enveloping them both with the burning glory of it.

"I love . . . you! I love . . . you!"

The Marquis had raised his lips from hers and now she could say it aloud, and she thought as she looked up at him that he had been transfigured into a man she had not seen before.

His air of cynicism and disdain had gone and he looked young, happy, and, she told herself, in love.

"How soon, my lovely darling, will you marry me?" he asked, and his voice was unsteady.

"What about . . . Peregrine?"

"He has already given us his blessing."

"You . . . told Peregrine you . . . wished to marry me?"

"I apologised to him humbly for the way I behaved. He was absolutely right in everything he said and everything he did!"

Neoma looked up in bewilderment.

Somehow it seemed impossible for the "Imperious Marquis" to apologise to anyone, least of all to her own brother!

"It is true," he said with a smile, "and Peregrine has already agreed to certain advantages which I have suggested to him as my future brother-in-law."

"What . . . are they?"

"I thought it would be wise for both him and Waddesdon to have something better to do than be let loose in London, spending money they do not possess."

"That is what I . . . thought."

"So I have suggested that I should buy them both commissions in my own Regiment the Life Guards."

Neoma gave a little cry.

"Do you . . . mean that? Do you really . . . mean it? It will mean everything to Peregrine—and he will be able to ride decent horses."

"I have a feeling," the Marquis answered, "that he will be riding mine as well, and I am glad you approve."

"Approve!" Neoma cried. "How can I thank you?"

"I will settle now for a kiss," the Marquis said tenderly, "but I still want to know the date of our wedding."

"Whenever you ... want," Neoma answered, moving a little nearer to him. "Tonight, tomorrow? I want ... to be ... with you."

The Marquis held her so tightly that she could barely breathe.

"That is what I want," he said. "I have wanted you to belong to me, my precious, since I first saw you."

"When was that?" Neoma asked.

"When you were standing by yourself in the Salon, looking so young, so beautiful, and so exceedingly pure."

"And you really thought I was the 'woman pure and fair' who did not exist?"

The Marquis gave a sigh.

"I was idiotic enough to suppose that you did not completely comply with what I desired, but that did not stop me from wanting you."

His arms tightened.

"When I found you in the Chapel I could not ..."

"How did you ... know I was ... there?" Neoma interrupted.

"I saw you running down the corridor as I came out of the Salon. I could not imagine what had happened."

"You must have ... thought I was ... half-witted to be so ... dense."

"Shall I tell you what I thought after you had gone to bed?"

Neoma looked at him anxiously.

"I thought, my precious little love, that I was the luckiest man in the world. I had found what all men seek in their hearts and so few find."

"You will not be ... disappointed?"

The Marquis smiled.

"I would have been in the darkness of despair if you had ceased to love me."

"How could I? You make me ... feel as if ... I have found a happiness so beautiful ... so wonderful ... it is not of this world."

The Marquis put his cheek against hers.

"Please," Neoma whispered, "will you explain ...

everything to me in the future so that I will not be so
. . . foolish . . . and ignorant?"

"I will tell you about love, my darling, but there
will be no need to know anything about other things,
because you will never again go to one of the Marquis of Rosyth's disreputable parties!"

"If I had not gone to one . . . I would never have
met you!"

The Marquis gave a little laugh.

"My precious—although I am deeply ashamed
that it ever happened—I shall always remember how
you looked at dinner that night!"

Neoma put her head against his shoulder.

"How . . . did I look?" she asked.

"Like an angel who had fallen from Heaven by
mistake, or perhaps it was a shadow on the light of the
moon. I did not know your name then."

He moved his lips over her skin as he went on:

"That is what you have to be for me in future—a
light to show me the way back to decency."

"Can I . . . really do that?"

"Only if you really love me."

"You know I do. I am yours, completely and
absolutely yours, although I did not . . . realise it until
you . . . kissed me."

"I will kiss you until I make you sure of it," the
Marquis answered.

Then his lips were on hers and there was music
and sunlight and the wonder that came from the Divine to envelop them with forgiveness for the past and
inspiration for the future.

"I love you! I love you!" Neoma said in her
heart.

She knew as she said it that it was also a prayer
that came from her soul.

Her prayers had been heard, and she thought
that her mother was very near her at this moment when
she had found a happiness so perfect, so exquisite, that
she wanted to go down on her knees and thank God for
it.

Instead, as she felt the Marquis's lips, fierce, de-
manding, and passionate, awakening the flame within

her which seemed to burn its way through her body, she vowed that she would dedicate herself to his happiness and make up to him for all he had suffered.

She realised that the scars were deep and it would be impossible for him to change overnight.

It was her sixth sense, her woman's perception, which made her see the difficulties ahead, the moments when the Marquis would still be disdainful and contemptuous.

Then she told herself that there were no difficulties, no problems that their love could not solve eventually.

As if growing, expanding, burning with a pure flame her love poured out towards him, evoking the response she wanted, he took his lips from hers to say:

"I love you! I adore you! Oh, my precious, wonderful little Light of the Moon, I cannot live without you, and you will guide me through our life together. You are mine—mine for all eternity."

Then there was only the glory of an indefinable ecstasy which lifted them both towards God.

ABOUT THE AUTHOR

BARBARA CARTLAND, the world's most famous romantic novelist, who is also an historian, playwright, lecturer, political speaker and television personality, has now written over 200 books.

She has also had many historical works published and has written four autobiographies as well as the biographies of her mother and that of her brother Ronald Cartland, who was the first Member of Parliament to be killed in the last war. This book has a preface by Sir Winston Churchill.

Barbara Cartland has sold 100 million books over the world, more than half of these in the U.S.A. She broke the world record in 1975 by writing twenty books, and her own record in 1976 with twenty-one. In addition, her album of love songs has just been published, sung with the Royal Philharmonic Orchestra.

In private life, Barbara Cartland, who is a Dame of the Order of St. John of Jerusalem, has fought for better conditions and salaries for Midwives and Nurses. As President of the Royal College of Midwives (Hertfordshire Branch), she has been invested with the first Badge of Office ever given in Great Britain, which was subscribed to by the Midwives themselves. She has also championed the cause for old people and founded the first Romany Gypsy Camp in the world.

Barbara Cartland is deeply interested in Vitamin Therapy and is President of the British National Association for Health.

BARBARA CARTLAND
PRESENTS
THE ANCIENT WISDOM SERIES

The world's all-time bestselling author of romantic fiction, Barbara Cartland, has established herself as High Priestess of Love in its purest and most traditionally romantic form.

"We have," she says, "in the last few years thrown out the spiritual aspect of love and concentrated only on the crudest and most debased sexual side.

"Love at its highest has inspired mankind since the beginning of time. Civilization's greatest pictures, music, prose and poetry have all been written under the influence of love. This love is what we all seek despite the temptations of the sensuous, the erotic, the violent and the perversions of pornography.

"I believe that for the young and the idealistic, my novels with their pure heroines and high ideals are a guide to happiness. Only by seeking the Divine Spark which exists in every human being, can we create a future built on the foundation of faith."

Barbara Cartland is also well known for her Library of Love, classic tales of romance, written by famous authors like Elinor Glyn and Ethel M. Dell, which have been personally selected and specially adapted for today's readers by Miss Cartland.

"These novels I have selected and edited for my 'Library of Love' are all stories with which the readers can identify themselves and also be assured that right will triumph in the end. These tales elevate and activate the mind rather than debase it as so many modern stories do."

Now, in August, Bantam presents the first four novels in a new Barbara Cartland Ancient Wisdom series. The books are THE FORBIDDEN CITY by Barbara Cartland, herself; THE ROMANCE OF TWO WORLDS by Marie Corelli; THE HOUSE OF FULFILLMENT by L. Adams Beck; and BLACK LIGHT by Talbot Mundy.

"Now I am introducing something which I think is of vital importance at this moment in history. Following my own autobiographical book I SEEK THE MIRACULOUS, which Dutton is publishing in hardcover this summer, I am offering those who seek 'the world behind the world' novels which contain, besides a fascinating story, the teaching of Ancient Wisdom.

"In the snow-covered vastnesses of the Himalayas, there are lamaseries filled with manuscripts which have been kept secret for century upon century. In the depths of the tropical jungles and the arid wastes of the deserts, there are also those who know the esoteric mysteries which few can understand.

"Yet some of their precious and sacred knowledge has been revealed to writers in the past. These books I have collected, edited and offer them to those who want to look beyond this greedy, grasping, materialistic world to find their own souls.

"I believe that Love, human and divine, is the jail-breaker of that prison of selfhood which confines and confuses us . . .

"I believe that for those who have attained enlightenment, super-normal (not super-human) powers are available to those who seek them."

All Barbara Cartland's own novels and her Library of Love are available in Bantam Books, wherever paperbacks are sold. Look for her Ancient Wisdom Series to be available in August.

Barbara Cartland

The world's bestselling author of romantic fiction.
Her stories are always captivating tales of intrigue,
adventure and love.

☐ 02972	A DREAM FROM THE NIGHT	$1.25
☐ 02987	CONQUERED BY LOVE	$1.25
☐ 10971	THE RHAPSODY OF LOVE	$1.50
☐ 10715	THE MARQUIS WHO HATED WOMEN	$1.50
☐ 10975	A DUEL WITH DESTINY	$1.50
☐ 10976	CURSE OF THE CLAN	$1.50
☐ 10977	PUNISHMENT OF A VIXEN	$1.50
☐ 11101	THE OUTRAGEOUS LADY	$1.50
☐ 11188	A TOUCH OF LOVE	$1.50
☐ 11169	THE DRAGON AND THE PEARL	$1.50
☐ 11962	A RUNAWAY STAR	$1.50
☐ 11690	PASSION AND THE FLOWER	$1.50
☐ 12292	THE RACE FOR LOVE	$1.50
☐ 12566	THE CHIEFTAIN WITHOUT A HEART	$1.50

Buy them at your local bookstore or use this handy coupon for ordering:

Barbara Cartland

The world's bestselling author of romantic fiction.
Her stories are always captivating tales of intrigue,
adventure and love.

☐	11372	LOVE AND THE LOATHSOME LEOPARD	$1.50
☐	11410	THE NAKED BATTLE	$1.50
☐	11512	THE HELL-CAT AND THE KING	$1.50
☐	11537	NO ESCAPE FROM LOVE	$1.50
☐	11580	THE CASTLE MADE FOR LOVE	$1.50
☐	11579	THE SIGN OF LOVE	$1.50
☐	11595	THE SAINT AND THE SINNER	$1.50
☐	11649	A FUGITIVE FROM LOVE	$1.50
☐	11797	THE TWISTS AND TURNS OF LOVE	$1.50
☐	11801	THE PROBLEMS OF LOVE	$1.50
☐	11751	LOVE LEAVES AT MIDNIGHT	$1.50
☐	11882	MAGIC OR MIRAGE	$1.50
☐	10712	LOVE LOCKED IN	$1.50
☐	11959	LORD RAVENSCAR'S REVENGE	$1.50
☐	11488	THE WILD, UNWILLING WIFE	$1.50
☐	11555	LOVE, LORDS, AND LADY-BIRDS	$1.50

Buy them at your local bookstore or use this handy coupon:

Barbara Cartland's Library of Love

The World's Great Stories of Romance Specially Abridged by Barbara Cartland For Today's Readers.